CHILDREN OF THE ALBATROSS

Children

of the Albatross

By Anaïs Nin

THE **SWALLOW PRESS** INC.

CHICAGO

Published by
The Swallow Press Incorporated
1139 South Wabash Avenue
Chicago, Illinois 60605

ISBN 0-8040-0039-5
LIBRARY OF CONGRESS CATALOG CARD NUMBER 66-6826

THE SEALED ROOM

STEPPING OFF the bus at Montmartre Djuna arrived in the center of the ambulant Fair and precisely at the moment when she set her right foot down on the cobblestones the music of the merry-go-round was unleashed from its mechanical box and she felt the whole scene, her mood, her body, transformed by its gaiety exactly as in her childhood her life in the orphan asylum had been suddenly transformed from a heavy nightmare to freedom by her winning of a dance scholarship.

As if, because of so many obstacles her childhood and adolescence had been painful, heavy walking on crutches and had suddenly changed overnight into a dance in which she discovered the air, space and the lightness of her own nature.

Her life was thus divided into two parts: the bare, the pedestrian one of her childhood, with poverty weighing her feet, and then the day when her interior monologue set to music led her feet into the dance.

Pointing her toe towards the floor she would always think: I danced my way out of the asylum, out of poverty, out of my past.

She remembered her feet on the bare floor of their first apartment. She remembered her feet on the linoleum of the orphan asylum. She remembered her feet going up and down the stairs of the home where she had been "adopted" and had suffered her jealousy of the affection bestowed on the legitimate children. She remembered her feet running away from that house.

She remembered her square-toed lusterless shoes, her mended stockings, and her hunger for new and shining shoes in shop windows.

She remembered the calluses on her feet from house work, from posing for painters, from working as a mannequin, from cold, from clumsy mendings and from ill-fitting shoes.

She remembered the day that her dreaming broke into singing, and became a monologue set to music, the day when the dreams became a miniature opera shutting out the harsh or dissonant sounds of the world.

She remembered the day when her feet became restless in their prison of lusterless leather and they began to vibrate in obedience to inner harmonizations, when she kicked off her shoes and as she moved her worn dress cracked under her arms and her skirt slit at the knees.

The flow of images set to music had descended from her head to her feet and she ceased to feel as one who had been split into two pieces by some great invisible saber cut.

In the external world she was the woman who had submitted to mysterious outer fatalities beyond her power to alter, and in her interior world she was a woman who had built many tunnels deeper down where no one could reach her, in which she deposited her treasures safe from destruction and in which she built a world exactly the opposite of the one she knew.

But at the moment of dancing a fusion took place, a welding, a wholeness. The cut in the middle of her body healed, and she was all one woman moving.

Lifted and impelled by an inner rhythm, with a music box playing inside her head, her foot lifted from drabness and immobility, from the swamps and miasmas of poverty, carried her across continents and oceans, depositing her on the cobblestones of a Paris square on the day of the Fair, among shimmering colored tents, the flags of pleasure at full mast, the merry-go-rounds turning like dervish dancers.

She walked to a side street, knocked on a dark doorway opened by a disheveled concierge and ran down the stairway to a vast underground room.

As she came down the stairway she could already hear the piano, feet stamping, and the ballet master's voice. When the piano stopped there was always his voice scolding, and the whispering of smaller voices.

Sometimes as she entered the class was dissolving, and a flurry of little girls brushed by her in their moth ballet costumes, the little girls from the Opera, laughing and whispering, fluttering like moths on their dusty ballet slippers, flurries of snow in the darkness of the vast room, with drops of dew from exertion.

Djuna went down with them along the corridors to the dressing rooms which at first looked like a garden, with the puffed white giant daisies of ballet skirts, the nasturtiums and poppies of Spanish skirts, the roses of cotton, the sunflowers, the spider webs of hair nets.

The small dressing room overflowed with the smell of cold cream, face powder, and cheap cologne, with the wild confusion of laughter, confessions from the girls, with old dancing slippers, faded flowers and withering tulle.

As soon as Djuna cast off her city clothes it was the trepidating moment of metamorphosis.

The piano slightly out of tune, the floor's vibrations, the odor of perspiration swelled the mood of excitement born in this garden of costumes to the accompaniment of whisperings and laughter.

When she extended her leg at the bar, the ballet master placed his hand on it as if to guide the accuracy of her pointed toe.

He was a slender, erect, stylized man of forty, not handsome in face; only in attitudes and gestures. His face was undefined, his features blurred. It was as if the dance were a sculptor who had taken hold of him and had carved style, form, elegance out of all his movements, but left the face unimportant.

She always felt his hand exceptionally warm whenever he placed it on her to guide, to correct, improve or change a gesture.

When he placed his hand on her ankle she became intensely aware of her ankle, as if he were the magician who caused the blood to flow through it; when he placed his hand on her waist she became intensely aware of her waist as if he were the sculptor who indented it.

When his hand gave the signal to dance then it was not only as if he had carved the form of her body and released the course of her blood but as if his hand had made the co-ordination between blood and gestures and form, and the *leçon de danse* became a lesson in living.

So she obeyed, she danced, she was flexible and yielding in his hands, plying her body, disciplining it, awakening it.

It became gradually apparent that she was the favorite.

11

She was the only one at whom he did not shout while she was dressing. He was more elated at her progress, and less harsh about her faults.

She obeyed his hands, but he found it more imperative than with other pupils to guide her by touch or by tender inflections of his voice.

He gave of his own movements as if he knew her movements would be better if he made them with her.

The dance gained in perfection, a perfection born of an accord between their gestures; born of her submission and his domination.

When he was tired she danced less well. When his attention was fixed on her she danced magnificently.

The little girls of the ballet troupe, mature in this experience, whispered and giggled: you are the favorite!

Yet not for a moment did he become for her a man. He was the ballet master. If he ruled her body with this magnetic rulership, a physical prestige, it was as a master of her dancing for the purpose of the dance.

But one day after the lessons, when the little girls from the Opera had left and there still hung in the air only an echo of the silk, flurry, snow and patter of activities, he followed her into the dressing room.

She had not yet taken off the voluminous skirt of the dance, the full-blown petticoat, the tight-fitting panties, so that when he entered the dressing room it seemed like a continuation of the dance. A continuation of the dance when he approached her and bent one knee in gallant salutation, and put his arms around her skirt that swelled like a huge flower. She laid her hand on his head like a queen acknowledging his worship. He remained on one knee while the skirt like a full-blown flower opened to allow a kiss to be placed at the core.

A kiss enclosed in the corolla of the skirt and hidden away, then he returned to the studio to speak with the pianist, to tell her at what time to come the next day, and to pay her, while Djuna dressed, covering warmth, covering her tremor, covering her fears.

He was waiting for her at the door, neat and trim.

He said: "Why don't you come and sit at the café with me?"

She followed him. Not far from there was the Place Clichy, always animated but more so now as the site of the Fair.

The merry-go-rounds were turning swiftly. The gypsies were reading fortunes in little booths hung with Arabian rugs.

Workman were shooting clay pigeons and winning cut-glass dishes for their wives.

The prostitutes were enjoying their watchful prome-nades, and the men their loitering.

The ballet master was talking to her: "Djuna (and suddenly as he said her name, she felt again where he had deposited his tribute), I am a simple man. My parents were shoemakers in a little village down south. I was put to work as a boy in an iron factory, where I handled heavy things and was on the way to becoming deformed by big muscles. But during my lunch hour I danced. I wanted to be a ballet dancer, and I practiced at one of the iron bars in front of a big furnace. And today—look!" He handed her a cigarette case all engraved with names of famous ballet dancers. "Today," he said proudly, "I have been the partner of all these women. If you would come with me, we could be happy. I am a simple man, but we could dance in all the cities of Europe. I am no longer young but I have a lot of dancing in me still. We could be happy. . . ."

The merry-go-round turned and her feelings with it, riding again the wooden horses of her childhood in the park, which was so much like flying, riding around from city to city reaching eagerly for the prizes, for bouquets, for clippings, for fame, flinging all of one's secret desires for pleasure on the outside like a red shawl, with this joyous music at the center always, the body recovered, the body dancing (hadn't she been the woman in quest of her body once lost by a shattering blow—submerged, and now floating again on the surface where uncrippled human beings lived in a world of pleasure like the Fair?).

How to explain to this simple man, how to explain. *There is something broken inside of me.* I cannot dance, live, love as easily as others. Surely enough, if we traveled around the world, I would break my leg somewhere, Because this inner break is invisible and unconvincing to others, I would not rest until I had broken something for everyone to see, to understand. How to explain to this simple man, I could not dance continuously with success, without breaking. *I am the dancer who falls*, always, into traps of depression, breaking my heart and my body almost at every turn, losing my tempo and my lightness, falling out of groups, out of grace, out of perfection. There is too often something wrong. Something you cannot help me with. . . . Supposing we found ourselves in a strange country, in a strange hotel. You are alone in a hotel room. Well, what of that? You can talk to the bar man, or you can sit before your glass of beer and read the papers. Everything is simple. But when I am alone in a hotel room something happens to me at times which must be what happens to children when the lights are turned out. Animals and children. But the animals howl their solitude, and children can call for their parents and for lights. But I. . . .

"What a long time it takes you to answer me," said the ballet master.

"I'm not strong enough," said Djuna.

"That's what I thought when I first saw you. I thought you couldn't take the discipline of a dancer's life. But it isn't so. You look fragile and all that, but you're healthy. I can tell healthy women by their skin. Yours is shining and clear. No, I don't think you have the strength of a horse, you're what we call 'une petite nature.' But you have energy and guts. And we'll take it easy on the road."

In the middle of a piece of music the merry-go-round suddenly stopped. Something had gone wrong with the motor! The horses slowed down their pace. The children lost their hilarity. The boss looked troubled, and the mechanic was called and like a doctor came with his bag.

The Fair lost its spinning frenzy.

When the music stopped, one could hear the dry shots of the amateur hunters and the clay pigeons falling behind the cardboard walls.

The dreams which Djuna had started to weave in the

16

asylum as if they were the one net in which she could exist, leaping thus always out of reach of unbearable happenings and creating her own events parallel to the ones her feelings could not accept, the dreams which gave birth to worlds within worlds, which, begun at night when she was asleep, continued during the day as an accompaniment to acts which she now discovered were rendered ineffectual by this defensive activity, with time became more and more violent.

For at first the personages of the dream, the cities which sprang up, were distinct and bore no resemblance to reality. They were images which filled her head with the vapors of fever, a drug-like panorama of incidents which rendered her insensible to cold, hunger and fatigue.

The day her mother was taken to the hospital to die, the day her brother was injured while playing in the street and developed a gentle insanity, the day at the asylum when she fell under the tyranny of the only man in the place, were days when she noted an intensification of her other world.

She could still weep at these happenings, but as people might lament just before they go under an anesthetic. "It still hurts," says the voice as the anesthetic begins to take effect and the pain growing duller, the body complaining more out of a mere remembrance of pain, automatically, just before sinking into a void.

She even found a way to master the weeping.

No mirrors were allowed in the orphan asylum, but girls had made one by placing black paper behind one of the small windows. Once a week they set it up and took turns at looking at their faces.

Djuna's first glimpse of the adolescent face was in this black mirror, where the clear coloring of her skin was as if touched with mourning, as if reflected at the bottom of a well.

Even long afterwards it was difficult for her to overcome this first impression of her face painted upon black still waters.

But she discovered that if she was weeping, and she looked at the weeping in a mirror, the weeping stopped. It ceased to be her own. It belonged to another.

Henceforth she possessed this power: whatever emotion would ravish or torment her, she could bring it before a mirror, look at it, and separate herself from it. And she thought she had found a way to master sorrow.

There was a boy of her age who passed every day under her window and who had the power to move her. He had a lean, eager face, eyes which seemed liquid with tenderness, and his gestures were full of gentleness.

His passage had the power to make her happy or un-happy, warm or cold, rich or poor. Whether he walked abstractedly on the other side of the street or on her side, whether he looked up at her window or forgot to look up, determined the mood of her day.

Because of his manner, she felt she trusted him en-tirely, that if he should come to the door and ask her to follow him she would do so without hesitation.

In her dreams at night she dissolved in his presence, lost herself in him. Her feelings for him were the opposite of an almost continuous and painful tension whose origin she did not know.

In contrast to this total submission to the unknown boy's gentleness, her first encounter with man was marked with defiance, fear, hostility.

The man, called the Watchman by the girls, was about forty years old when Djuna was sixteen. He was possessed of unlimited power because he was the lover of the Directress. His main attribute was power. He was the only man in the asylum, and he could deal privileges, gifts, and give permissions to go out at night.

This unique role gave him a high prestige. He was polite, carried himself with confidence, and was hand-some in a neutral way which adapted him easily to any kind of image the orphans wished to fashion of him.

He could pass for the tall man, the brown-haired man, the blond man; given a little leeway, he answered all the descriptions of gypsy card readers.

An added piquancy was attained by the common knowledge that he was the favorite of the Directress, who was very much hated. In winning his favor, one struck indirect blows at her authority, and achieved a subtle revenge for her severity.

The girls thought of him as possessing an even greater power than hers, for she who submitted to no one, had often been seen bowing her head before his reproaches.

The one he chose felt endowed immediately with greater beauty, greater charm and power than the other girls. He was appointed the arbiter, the connoisseur, the bestower of decorations.

To be chosen by the Watchman was to enter the realm of protection. No girl could resist this.

Djuna could distinguish his steps at a great distance. It seemed to her that he walked more evenly than anyone she knew, evenly and without stops or change of rhythm. He advanced through the hallways inexorably. Other people could be stopped, or eluded. But his steps were those of absolute authority.

He knew at what time Djuna would be passing

through this particular hallway alone. He always came up to her, not a yard away, but exactly beside her.

His glance was always leveled at her breasts, and two things would happen simultaneously: he would offer her a present without looking at her face, as if he were offering it to her breasts, and then he would whisper: "Tonight I will let you out if you are good to me."

And Djuna would think of the boy who passed by under her window, and feel a wild beating of her heart at the possibility of meeting him outside, of talking to him, and her longing for the boy, for the warm liquid tenderness of his eyes was so violent that no sacrifice seemed too great—her longing and her feeling that if he knew of this scene, he would rescue her, but that there was no other way to reach him, no other way to defeat authority to reach him than by this concession to authority.

In this barter there was no question of rebellion. The way the Watchman stood, demanded, gestured, was all part of a will she did not even question, a continuation of the will of the father. There was the man who demanded, and outside was the gentle boy who demanded nothing, and to whom she wanted to give everything, whose silence even, she trusted, whose way of walking she trusted with her entire heart, while this man she did not trust.

It was the *droit du seigneur*.

She slipped the Watchman's bracelet around the lusterless cotton of her dress, while he said: "The poorer the dress the more wonderful your skin looks, Djuna."

Years later when Djuna thought the figure of the Watchman was long since lost she would hear echoes of his heavy step and she would find herself in the same mood she had experienced so many times in his presence.

No longer a child, and yet many times she still had the feeling that she might be overpowered by a will stronger than her own, might be trapped, might be somehow unable to free herself, unable to escape the demands of man upon her.

Her first defeat at the hands of man the father had caused her such a conviction of helplessness before tyranny that although she realized that she was now in reality no longer helpless, the echo of this helplessness was so strong that she still dreaded the possessiveness and willfullness of older men. They benefited from this regression into her past, and could override her strength merely because of this conviction of unequal power.

It was as if maturity did not develop altogether and completely, but by little compartments like the airtight sections of a ship. A part of her being would mature, such as her insight, or interpretative faculties, but another could retain a childhood conviction that events, man and authority together were stronger than one's capacity for mastering them, and that one was doomed to become a victim of one's pattern.

It was only much later that Djuna discovered that this belief in the greater power of others became the fate itself and caused the defeats.

But for years, she felt harmed and defeated at the hands of men of power, and she expected the boy, the gentle one, the trusted one, to come and deliver her from tyranny.

Ever since the day of Lillian's concert when she had seen the garden out of the window, Djuna had wanted a garden like it.

And now she possessed a garden and a very old house on the very edge of Paris, between the city and the Park.

But it was not enough to possess it, to walk through it, sit in it. One still had to be able to live in it.

And she found she could not live in it.

The inner fever, the restlessness within her corroded her life in the garden.

When she was sitting in a long easy chair she was not at ease.

The grass seemed too much like a rug awaiting footsteps, to be trampled with hasty incidents. The rhythm of growth too slow, the falling of the leaves too tranquil.

Happiness was an absence of fever. The garden was feverless and without tension to match her tensions. She could not unite or commune with the plants, the languor, the peace. It was all contrary to her inward pulse. Not one pulsation of the garden corresponded to her inner pulsation which was more like a drum beating feverish time.

Within her the leaves did not wait for autumn, but were torn off prematurely by unexpected sorrows. Within her, leaves did not wait for spring to sprout but bloomed in sudden hothouse exaggerations. Within her there were storms contrary to the lazy moods of the garden, devastations for which nature had no equivalent.

Peace, said the garden, peace.

The day began always with the sound of crushed gravel by the automobiles.

The shutters were pushed open by the French servant, and the day admitted.

With the first crushing of the gravel under wheels came the barking of the police dog and the carillon of the church bells.

Cars entered through an enormous green iron gate,

which had to be opened ceremoniously by the servant.

Everyone else walked through the small green gate that seemed like the child of the other, half covered with ivy. The ivy did not climb over the father gate.

When Djuna looked at the large gate through her window it took on the air of a prison gate. An unjust feeling, since she knew she could leave the place whenever she wanted, and since she knew more than anyone that human beings placed upon an object, or a person this responsibility of being the obstacle, when the obstacle lay within one's self.

In spite of this knowledge, she would often stand at the window staring at the large closed iron gate as if hoping to obtain from this contemplation a reflection of her inner obstacles to a full open life.

She mocked its importance; the big gate had a presumptuous creak! Its rusty voice was full of dissonant affectations. No amount of oil could subdue its rheumatism, for it took a historical pride in its own rust: it was a hundred years old.

But the little gate, with its overhanging ivy like disordered hair over a running child's forehead, had a sleepy and sly air, an air of always being half open, never entirely locked.

Djuna had chosen the house for many reasons, because

it seemed to have sprouted out of the earth like a tree, so deeply grooved it was within the old garden. It had no cellar and the rooms rested right on the ground. Below the rugs, she felt, was the earth. One could take root here, feel at one with the house and garden, take nourishment from them like the plants.

She had chosen it too because its symmetrical façade covered by a trellis overrun by ivy showed twelve window faces. But one shutter was closed and corresponded to no room. During some transformation of the house it had been walled up.

Djuna had taken the house because of this window which led to no room, because of this impenetrable room, thinking that someday she would discover an entrance to it.

In front of the house there was a basin which had been filled, and a well which had been sealed up. Djuna set about restoring the basin, excavated an old fountain and unsealed the well.

Then it seemed to her that the house came alive, the flow was re-established.

The fountain was gay and sprightly, the well deep.

The front half of the garden was trim and stylized like most French gardens, but the back of it some past owner had allowed to grow wild and become a miniature jungle. The stream was almost hidden by overgrown plants, and the small bridge seemed like a Japanese bridge in a glass-bowl garden.

There was a huge tree of which she did not know the name, but which she named the Ink Tree for its black and poisonous berries.

One summer night she stood in the courtyard. All the windows of the house were lighted.

Then the image of the house with all its windows lighted—all but one—she saw as the image of the self, of the being divided into many cells. Action taking place in one room, now in another, was the replica of experience taking place in one part of the being, now in another.

The room of the heart in Chinese lacquer red, the room of the mind in pale green or the brown of philosophy, the room of the body in shell rose, the attic of memory with closets full of the musk of the past.

She saw the whole house on fire in the summer night and it was like those moments of great passion and deep experience when every cell of the self lighted simultaneously, a dream of fullness, and she hungered for this that would set aflame every room of the house and of herself at once!

In herself there was one shuttered window.

She did not sleep soundly in the old and beautiful house.

She was disturbed.

She could hear voices in the dark, for it is true that on days of clear audibility there are voices which come from within and speak in multiple tongues contradicting each other. They speak out of the past, out of the present, the voices of awareness—in dialogues with the self which mark each step of living.

There was the voice of the child in herself, unburied, who had long ago insisted: I want only the marvelous.

There was the low-toned and simple voice of the human being Djuna saying: I want love.

There was the voice of the artist in Djuna saying: I will create the marvelous.

Why should such wishes conflict with each other, or annihilate each other?

In the morning the human being Djuna sat on the carpet before the fireplace and mended and folded her stockings into little partitioned boxes, keeping the one perfect unmended pair for a day of high living, partitioning at the same time events into little separate boxes in her head, dividing (that was one of the great secrets against shattering sorrows) allotting and rearranging under the heading of one word a constantly fluid, mobile

28

and protean universe whose multiple aspects were like quicksands.

This exaggerated sense, for instance, of a preparation for the love to come, like the extension of canopies, the unrolling of ceremonial carpets, the belief in the state of grace, of a perfection necessary to the advent of love.

As if she must first of all create a marvelous world in which to house it, thinking it befell her adequately to receive this guest of honor.

Wasn't it too oriental, said a voice protesting with mockery—such elaborate receptions, such costuming, as if love were such an exigent guest?

She was like a perpetual bride perparing a trousseau. As other women sew and embroider, or curl their hair, she embellished her cities of the interior, painted, decorated, prepared a great *mise en scène* for a great love.

It was in this mood of preparation that she passed through her kingdom the house, painting here a wall through which the stains of dampness showed, hanging a lamp where it would throw Balinese theater shadows, draping a bed, placing logs in the fireplaces, wiping the dull-surfaced furniture that it might shine. Every room in a different tone like the varied pipes of an organ, to emit a wide range of moods—lacquer red for vehemence, gray for confidences, a whole house of moods with many doors, passageways, and changes of level.

She was not satisfied until it emitted a glow which was not only that of the Dutch interiors in Dutch paintings, a glow of immaculateness, but an effulgence which had caused Jay to dissert on the gold dust of Florentine paintings.

Djuna would stand very still and mute and feel: my house will speak for me. My house will tell them I am warm and rich. The house will tell them inside of me there are these rooms of flesh and Chinese lacquer, sea greens to walk through, inside of me there are lighted candles, live fires, shadows, spaces, open doors, shelters and air currents. Inside of me there is color and warmth.

The house will speak for me.

People came and submitted to her spell, but like all spells it was wonderful and remote. Not warm and near. No human being, they thought, made this house, no human being lived here. It was too fragile and too unfamiliar. There was no dust on her hands, no broken nails, no sign of wear and tear.

It was the house of the myth.

It was the ritual they sensed, tasted, smelled. Too different from the taste and smell of their own houses. It took them out of the present. They took on an air of temporary guests. No familiar landscape, no signpost to say: this is your home as well.

All of them felt they were passing, could not remain. They were tourists visiting foreign lands. It was a voyage and not a port.

Even in the bathroom there were no medicine bottles on the shelves proclaiming: soda, castor oil, cold cream. She had transferred all of them to alchemist bottles, and the homeliest drug assumed an air of philter.

This was a dream and she was merely a guide.

None came near enough.

There were houses, dresses, which created one's isolation as surely as those tunnels created by ferrets to elude pursuit of the male.

There were rooms and costumes which appeared to be made to lure but which were actually effective means to create distance.

Djuna had not yet decided what her true wishes were, or how near she wanted them to come. She was apparently calling to them but at the same time, by a great ambivalence and fear of their coming too near, of invading her, of dominating or possessing her, she was charming them in such a manner that the human being in her, the warm and simple human being, remained secure from invasion. She constructed a subtle obstacle to invasion

31

at the same time as she constructed an appealing scene.

None came near enough. After they left she sat alone, and deserted, as lonely as if they had not come.

She was alone as everyone is every morning after a dream.

What was this that was weeping inside of her costume and house, something smaller and simpler than the edifice of spells?

She did not know why she was left hungry.

The dream took place. Everything had contributed to its perfection, even her silence, for she would not speak when she had nothing meaningful to say (like the silence in dreams between fateful events and fateful phrases, never a trivial word spoken in dreams!).

The next day, unknowing, she began anew.

She poured medicines from ugly bottles into alchemist bottles, creating minor mysteries, minor transmutations.

Insomnia. The nights were long.

Who would come and say: that is *my* dream, and take up the thread and make all the answers?

Or are all dreams made alone?

Lying in the fevered sheets of insomnia, there was a human being cheated by the dream.

Insomnia came when one must be on the watch, when one awaited an important visitor.

Everyone, Djuna felt, saw the dancer on light feet but no one seized the moment when she vacillated, fell. No one perceived or shared her difficulties, the mere technical difficulties of loving, dancing, believing.

When she fell, she fell alone, as she had in adolescence.

She remembered feeling this mood as a girl, that all her adolescence had proceeded by oscillations between weakness and strength. She remembered, too, that whenever she became entangled in too great a difficulty she had these swift regressions into her adolescent state. Almost as if in the large world of maturity, when the obstacle loomed too large, she shrank again into the body of the young girl for whom the world had first appeared as a violent and dangerous place, forcing her to retreat, and when she retreated she fell back into smallness.

She returned to the adolescent deserts of mistrust of love.

Walking through snow, carrying her muff like an obsolete wand no longer possessed of the power to create the personage she needed, she felt herself walking through a desert of snow.

Her body muffled in furs, her heart muffled like her steps, and the pain of living muffled as by the deepest rich carpets, while the thread of Ariadne which led everywhere, right and left, like scattered footsteps in the snow, tugged and pulled within her memory and she began to pull upon this thread (silk for the days of marvel and cotton for the bread of everyday living which was always a little stale) as one pulls upon a spool, and she heard the empty wooden spool knock against the floor of different houses.

Holding the silk or cotton began to cut her fingers which bled from so much unwinding, or was it that the thread of Ariadne had led into a wound?

The thread slipped through her fingers now, with blood on it, and the snow was no longer white.

Too much snow on the spool she was unwinding from the tightly wound memories. Unwinding snow as it lay thick and hard around the edges of her adolescence because the desire of men did not find a magical way to open her being.

The only words which opened her being were the muffled words of poets so rarely uttered by human beings. They alone penetrated her without awakening the bristling guards on watch at the gateways, costumed like silver porcupines armed with mistrust, barring the way to the secret recesses of her thoughts and feelings.

Before most people, most places, most situations, most words, Djuna's being, at sixteen, closed hermetically into muteness. The sentinels bristled: someone is approaching! And all the passages to her inner self would close.

Today as a mature woman she could see how these sentinels had not been content with defending her, but they had constructed a veritable fort under this mask of gentle shyness, forts with masked holes concealing weapons built by fear.

The snow accumulated every night all around the rim of her young body.

Blue and crackling snowbound adolescence.

The young men who sought to approach her then, drawn by her warm eyes, were startled to meet with such harsh resistance.

This was no mere flight of coquetry inviting pursuit. It was a fort of snow (for the snowbound, dream-swallower of the frozen fairs). An unmeltable fort of timidity.

Yet each time she walked, muffled, protected, she was aware of two women walking: one intent on creating trap doors of evasion, the other wishing someone might find the entrance that she might not be so alone.

With Michael it was as if she had not heard him coming, so gentle were his steps, his words. Not the walk or words of the hunter, of the man of war, the determined entrance of older men, not the dominant walk of the father, the familiar walk of the brother, not like any other man she knew.

Only a year older than herself, he walked into her blue and white climate with so light a tread that the guards did not hear him!

He came into the room with a walk of vulnerability, treading softly as upon a carpet of delicacies. He would not crush the moss, no gravel would complain under his feet, no plant would bow its head or break.

It was a walk like a dance in which the gentleness of the steps carried him through air, space and silence in a sentient minuet in accord with his partner's mood, his leaf-green eyes obeying every rhythm, attentive to harmony, fearful of discord, with an excessive care for the other's intent.

The path his steps took, his velvet words, miraculously slipped between the bristles of her mistrust, and before she had been fully aware of his coming, by his softness he had entered fully into the blue and white climate.

The mists of adolescence were not torn open, not even disturbed by his entrance.

He came with poems, with worship, with flowers not ordered from the florist but picked in the forest near his school.

He came not to plunder, to possess, to overpower.

36

With great gentleness he moved towards the hospitable regions of her being, towards the peaceful fields of her interior landscape, where white flowers placed themselves against green backgrounds as in Botticelli paintings of spring.

At his entrance her head remained slightly inclined towards the right, as it was when she was alone, slightly weighed down by pensiveness, whereas on other occasions, at the least approach of a stranger, her head would raise itself tautly in preparation for danger.

And so he entered into the flowered regions behind the forts, having easily crossed all the moats of politeness.

His blond hair gave him the befitting golden tones attributed to most legendary figures.

Djuna never knew whether this light of sun he emitted came out of his own being or was thrown upon him by her dream of him, as later she had observed the withdrawal of this light from those she had ceased to love. She never knew whether two people woven together by feelings answering each other as echoes threw off a phosphorescence, the chemical sparks of marriage, or whether each one threw upon the other the spotlight of his inner dream.

Transient or everlasting, inner or outer, personal or

magical, there was now this lighting falling upon both of them and they could only see each other in its spanning circle which dazzled them and separated them from the rest of the world.

Through the cocoon of her shyness her voice had been hardly audible, but he heard every shading of it, could follow its nuances even when it retreated into the furthest impasse of the ear's labyrinth.

Secretive and silent in relation to the world, she became exalted and intense once placed inside of this inner circle of light.

This light which enclosed two was familiar and natural to her.

Because of their youth, and their moving still outside of the center of their own desires blindly, what they danced together was not a dance in which either took possession of the other, but a kind of minuet, where the aim consisted in *not* appropriating, *not* grasping, *not* touching, but allowing the maximum space and distance to flow between the two figures. To move in accord without collisions, without merging. To encircle, to bow in worship, to laugh at the same absurdities, to mock their own movements, to throw upon the walls twin shadows which will never become one. To dance around this danger: the danger of becoming one! To dance keeping each to his own path. To allow parallelism, but no loss of the self into the other. To play at marriage, step by step, to read the same book together, to dance a dance of elusiveness on the rim of desire, to remain within circles of heightened lighting without touching the core that would set the circle on fire.

A deft dance of unpossession.

They met once at a party, imprinted on each other forever the first physical image: she saw him tall, with an easy bearing, an easily flowing laughter. She saw all: the ivory color of the skin, the gold metal sheen of the hair, the lean body carved with meticulous economy as for racing, running, leaping; tender fingers touching objects as if all the world were fragile; tender inflections of the voice without malice or mockery; eyelashes always ready to fall over the eyes when people spoke harshly around him.

He absorbed her dark, long, swinging hair, the blue eyes never at rest, a little slanted, quick to close their curtains too, quick to laugh, but more often thirsty, absorbing like a mirror. She allowed the pupil to receive these images of others but one felt they did not vanish altogether as they would on a mirror: one felt a thirsty being absorbing reflections and drinking words and faces into herself for a deep communion with them.

She never took up the art of words, the art of talk. She remained always as Michael had first seen her: a woman who talked with her Naiad hair, her winged eyelashes, her tilted head, her fluent waist and rhetorical feet.

She never said: I have a pain. But laid her two arms over the painful area as if to quieten a rebellious child, rocking and cradling this angry nerve. She never said: I am afraid. But entered the room on tiptoes, her eyes watching for ambushes.

She was already the dancer she was to become, eloquent with her body.

They met once and then Michael began to write her letters as soon as he returned to college.

In these letters he appointed her Isis and Arethusa, Iseult and the Seven Muses.

Djuna became the woman with the face of all women.

With strange omissions: he was neither Osiris nor Tristram, nor any of the mates or pursuers.

He became uneasy when she tried to clothe *him* in the costume of myth figures.

When he came to see her during vacations they never touched humanly, not even by a handclasp. It was as if they had found the most intricate way of communicating with each other by way of historical personages, literary passions, and that any direct touch even of finger tips would explode this world.

With each substitution they increased the distance between their human selves.

Djuna was not alarmed. She regarded this with feminine eyes: in creating this world Michael was merely constructing a huge, superior, magnificent nest in some mythological tree, and one day he would ask her to step into it with him, carrying her over the threshold all costumed in the trappings of his fantasy, and he would say: this is our home!

All this to Djuna was an infinitely superior way of wooing her, and she never doubted its ultimate purpose, or climax, for in this the most subtle women are basically simple and do not consider mythology or symbolism as a substitute for the climaxes of nature, merely as adornments!

This mist of adolescence, prolonging and expanding the wooing, was merely an elaboration of the courtship. His imagination continued to create endless detours as if they had to live first of all through all the loves of history and fiction before they could focus on their own.

But the peace in his moss-green eyes disturbed her, for

41

in her eyes there now glowed a fever. Her breasts hurt her at night, as if from overfullness.

His eyes continued to focus on the most distant points of all, but hers began to focus on the near, the present. She would dwell on a detail of his face. On his ears for instance. On the movements of his lips when he talked. She failed to hear some of his words because she was following with her eyes and her feelings the contours of his lips moving as if they were moving on the surface of her skin.

She began to understand for the first time the carnation in Carmen's mouth. Carmen was eating the mock orange of love: the white blossoms which she bit were like skin. Her lips had pressed around the mock-orange petals of desire.

In Djuna all the moats were annihilated: she stood perilously near to Michael glowing with her own natural warmth. Days of clear visibility which Michael did not share. His compass still pointed to the remote, the unknown.

Djuna was a woman being dreamed.

But Djuna had ceased to dream: she had tasted the mock orange of desire.

More baffling still to Djuna grown warm and near, with her aching breasts, was that the moss-green serenity of Michael's eyes was going to dissolve into jealousy without pausing at desire.

He took her to a dance. His friends eagerly appropriated her. From across the room full of dancers, for the first time he saw not her eyes but her mouth, as vividly as she had seen his. Very clear and very near, and he felt the taste of it upon his lips.

For the first time, as she danced away from him, encircled by young men's arms, he measured the great space they had been swimming through, measured it exactly as others measure the distance between planets.

The mileage of space he had put between himself and Djuna. The lighthouse of the eyes alone could traverse such immensity!

And now, after such elaborations in space, so many figures interposed between them, the white face of Iseult, the burning face of Catherine, all of which he had interpreted as mere elaborations of his enjoyment of her, now suddenly appeared not as ornaments but as obstructions to his possession of her.

She was lost to him now. She was carried away by other young men, turning with them. They had taken her waist as he never had, they bent her, plied her to the movements of the dance, and she answered and responded: they were mated by the dance.

As she passed him he called out her name severely, reproachfully, and Djuna saw the green of his eyes turned to violet with jealousy.

"Djuna! I'm taking you home."

For the first time he was willful, and she liked it.

"Djuna!" He called again, angrily, his eyes darkening with anger.

She had to stop dancing. She came gently towards him, thinking: "He wants me all to himself," and she was happy to yield to him.

He was only a little taller than she was, but he held himself very erect and commanding.

On the way home he was silent.

The design of her mouth had vanished again, his journey towards her mouth had ceased the moment it came so near in reality to his own. It was as if he dared to experience a possibility of communion only while the obstacle to it was insurmountable, but as the obstacle was removed and she walked clinging to his arm, then he could only commune with her eyes, and the distance was again reinstated.

He left her at her door without a sign of tenderness, with only the last violet shadows of jealousy lurking reproachfully in his eyes. That was all.

Djuna sobbed all night before the mystery of his jealousy, his anger, his remoteness.

She would not question him. He confided nothing. They barred all means of communication with each other. He would not tell her that at this very dance he had discovered an intermediate world from which all the figures of women were absent. A world of boys like himself in flight away from woman, mother, sister, wife or mistress.

In her ignorance and innocence then, she could not have pierced with the greatest divination where Michael, in his flight from her, gave his desire.

In their youthful blindness they wounded each other. He excused his coldness towards her: "You're too slender. I like plump women." Or again: "You're too intelligent. I feel better with stupid women." Or another time he said: "You're too impulsive, and that frightens me."

Being innocent, she readily accepted the blame.

Strange scenes took place between them. She subdued her intelligence and became passive to please him. But it was a game, and they both knew it. Her ebullience broke through all her pretenses at quietism.

She swallowed countless fattening pills, but could

only gain a pound or two. When she proudly asked him to note the improvements, his eyes turned away.

One day he said: "I feel your clever head watching me, and you would look down on me if I failed."

Failed?

She could not understand.

With time, her marriage to another, her dancing which took her to many countries, the image of Michael was effaced.

But she continued to relate to other Michaels in the world. Some part of her being continued to recognize the same gentleness, the same elusiveness, the same mystery.

Michael reappeared under different bodies, guises, and each time she responded to him, discovering each time a little more until she pierced the entire mystery open.

But the same little dance took place each time, a little dance of insolence, a dance which said to the woman: "I dance alone, I will not be possessed by a woman."

The kind of dance tradition had taught woman as a ritual to provoke aggression! But this dance made by young men before the women left them at a loss for it was not intended to be answered.

———

Years later she sat a café table in Paris between Michael and Donald.

Why should she be sitting between Michael and Donald?

Why were not all cords cut between herself and Michael when she married and when he gave himself to a succession of Donalds?

When they met in Paris again, he had this need to invent a trinity: to establish a connecting link between Djuna and all the changing, fluctuating Donalds.

As if some element were lacking in his relation to Donald.

Donald had a slender body, like an Egyptian boy. Dark hair wild like that of a child who had been running. At moments the extreme softness of his gestures made him appear small, at others when he stood stylized and pure in line, erect, he seemed tall and firm.

His eyes were large and entranced, and he talked flowingly like a medium. His eyelids fell heavily over his eyes like a woman's, with a sweep of the eyelashes. He had a small straight nose, small ears, and strong boyish hands.

When Michael left for cigarettes they looked at each other, and immediately Donald ceased to be a woman.

He straightened his body and looked at Djuna un-flinchingly.

With her he asserted his strength. Was it her being a woman which challenged his strength? He was now like a grave child in the stage of becoming a man.

With the smile of a conspirator he said: "Michael treats me as if I were a woman or a child. He wants me not to work and to depend on him. He wants to go and live down south in a kind of paradise."

"And what do you want?"

"I am not sure I love Michael. . . ."

That was exactly what she expected to hear. Always this admission of incompleteness. Always one in flight or the three sitting together, always one complaining or one loving less than the other.

All this accompanied by the most complicated har-monization of expressions Djuna had ever seen. The eyes and mouth of Donald suggesting an excitement familiar to drug addicts, only in Donald it did not derive from any artificial drugs but from the strange flavor he extracted from difficulties, from the maze and detours and unfulfillments of his loves.

In Donald's eyes shone the fever of futile watches in the night, intrigue, pursuits of the forbidden, all the rhythms and moods unknown to ordinary living. There was a quest for the forbidden and it was this flavor he sought, as well as the strange lighting which fell on all the unknown, the unfamiliar, the tabooed, all that could remind him of those secret moments of childhood when he sought the very experiences most forbidden by the parents.

But when it came to the selection of one, to giving one's self to one, to an open simplicity and an effort at completeness, some mysterious impulse always intervened and destroyed the relationship. A hatred of permanency, of anything resembling marriage.

Donald was talking against Michael's paradise as it would destroy the bitter-sweet, intense flavor he sought.

He bent closer to Djuna, whispering now like a conspirator. It was his conspiracy against simplicity, against Michael's desire for a peaceful life together.

"If you only knew, Djuna, the first time it happened! I expected the whole world to change its face, be utterly transformed, turned upside down. I expected the room to become inclined, as after an earthquake, to find that the door no longer led to a stairway but into space, and the windows overlooked the sea. Such excitement, such anxiety, and such a fear of not achieving fulfillment. At other times I have the feeling that I am escaping a prison, I have a fear of being caught again and punished.

When I signal to another like myself in a café I have the feeling that we are two prisoners who have found a laborious way to communicate by a secret code. All our messages are colored with the violent colors of danger. What I find in this devious way has a taste like no other object overtly obtained. Like the taste of those dim and secret afternoons of our childhood when we performed forbidden acts with great anxiety and terror of punishment. The exaltation of danger, I'm used to it now, the fever of remorse. This society which condemns me . . . do you know how I am revenging myself? I am seducing each one of its members slowly, one by one. . . ."

He talked softly and exultantly, choosing the silkiest words, not disguising his dream of triumphing over all those who had dared to forbid certain acts, and certain forms of love.

At the same time when he talked about Michael there came to his face the same expression women have when they have seduced a man, an expression of vain glee, a triumphant, uncontrollable celebration of her power. And so Donald was celebrating the feminine wiles and ruses and charms by which he had made Michael fall so deeply in love with him.

In his flight from woman, it seemed to Djuna, Michael had merely fled to one containing all the minor flaws of women.

Donald stopped talking and there remained in the air the feminine intonations of his voice, chanting and never falling into deeper tones.

Michael was back and sat between them offering cigarettes.

As soon as Michael returned Djuna saw Donald change, become woman again, tantalizing and provocative. She saw Donald's body dilating into feminine undulations, his face open in all nakedness. His face expressed a dissolution like that of a woman being taken. Everything revealed, glee, the malice, the vanity, the childishness. His gestures like those of a second-rate actress receiving flowers with a batting of the eyelashes, with an oblique glance like the upturned cover of a bedspread, the edge of a petticoat.

He had the stage bird's turns of the head, the little dance of alertness, the petulance of the mouth pursed for small kisses that do not shatter the being, the flutter and perk of prize birds, all adornment and change, a mockery of the evanescent darts of invitation, the small gestures of alarm and promise made by minor women.

Michael said: "You two resemble each other. I am sure Donald's suits would fit you, Djuna."

"But Donald is more truthful," said Djuna, thinking how openly Donald betrayed that he did not love

Michael, whereas she might have sought a hundred oblique routes to soften this truth.

"Donald is more truthful because he loves less," said Michael.

Warmth in the air. The spring foliage shivering out of pure coquetry, not out of discomfort. Love flowing now between the three, shared, transmitted, contagious, as if Michael were at last free to love Djuna in the form of a boy, through the body of Donald to reach Djuna whom he could never touch directly, and Djuna through the body of Donald reached Michael—and the missing dimension of their love accomplished in space like an algebra of imperfection, an abstract drama of incompleteness at last resolved for one moment by this trinity of woman sitting between two incomplete men.

She could look with Michael's eyes at Donald's finely designed body, the narrow waist, the square shoulders, the stylized gestures and dilated expression.

She could see that Donald did not give his true self to Michael. He acted for him a caricature of woman's minor petulances and caprices. He ordered a drink and then changed his mind, and when the drink came he did not want it at all.

Djuna thought: "He is like a woman without the

womb in which such great mysteries take place. He is a travesty of a marriage that will never take place."

Donald rose, performed a little dance of salutation and flight before them, eluding Michael's pleading eyes, bowed, made some whimsical gesture of apology and flight, and left them.

This little dance reminded her of Michael's farewells on her doorsteps when she was sixteen.

And suddenly she saw all their movements, hers with Michael, and Michael's with Donald, as a ballet of unreality and unpossession.

"Their greatest form of activity is flight!" she said to Michael.

To the tune of Debussy's *Ile Joyeuse*, they gracefully made all the steps which lead to no possession.

(When will I stop loving these airy young men who move in a realm like the realm of the birds, always a little quicker than most human beings, always a little above, or beyond humanity, always in flight, out of some great fear of human beings, always seeking the open space, wary of enclosures, anxious for their freedom, vibrating with a multitude of alarms, always sensing danger all around them. . . .)

"Birds," said a research scientist, "live their lives with

an intensity as extreme as their brilliant colors and their vivid songs. Their body temperatures are regularly as high as 105 to 110 degrees, and anyone who has watched a bird at close range must have seen how its whole body vibrates with the furious pounding of its pulse. Such engines must operate at forced draft: and that is exactly what a bird does. The bird's indrawn breath not only fills its lungs, but also passes on through myriads of tiny tubules into air sacs that fill every space in the bird's body not occupied by vital organs. Furthermore the air sacs connect with many of the bird's bones, which are not filled with marrow as animals' bones are, but are hollow. These reserve air tanks provide fuel for the bird's intensive life, and at the same time add to its buoyancy in flight."

Paul arrived as the dawn arrives, mist-laden, uncertain of his gestures. The sun was hidden until he smiled. Then the blue of his eyes, the shadows under his eyes, the sleepy eyelids, were all illuminated by the wide, brilliant smile. Mist, dew, the uncertain hoverings of his gestures were dispelled by the full, firm mouth, the strong even teeth.

Then the smile vanished again, as quickly as it had come. When he entered her room he brought with him this climate of adolescence which is neither sun nor full moon but the intermediate regions.

Again she noticed the shadows under his eyes, which made a soft violet-tinted halo around the intense blue of the pupils.

He was mantled in shyness, and his eyelids were heavy as if from too much dreaming. His dreaming lay like the edges of a deep slumber on the rim of his eyelids. One expected them to close in a hypnosis of interior fantasy as mysterious as a drugged state.

This constant passing from cloudedness to brilliance took place within a few instants. His body would sit absolutely still, and then would suddenly leap into gaiety and lightness. Then once again his face would close hermetically.

He passed in the same quick way between phrases uttered with profound maturity to sudden innocent inaccuracies.

It was difficult to remember he was seventeen.

He seemed more preoccupied with uncertainty as to how to carry himself through this unfamiliar experience than with absorbing or enjoying it.

Uncertainty spoiled his pleasure in the present, but Djuna felt he was one to carry away his treasures into secret chambers of remembrance and there he would lay them all out like the contents of an opium pipe being prepared, these treasures no longer endangered by uneasiness in living, the treasures becoming the past, and there he would touch and caress every word, every image, and make them his own.

In solitude and remembrance his real life would begin. Everything that was happening now was merely the preparation of the opium pipe that would later send volutes into space to enchant his solitude, when he would be lying down away from danger and unfamiliarity, lying down to taste of an experience washed of the dross of anxiety.

He would lie down and nothing more would be demanded of the dreamer, no longer expected to participate, to speak, to act, to decide. He would lie down and the images would rise in chimerical visitations and form a tale more marvelous in every detail than the one taking place at this moment marred by apprehension.

Having created a dream beforehand which he sought to preserve from destruction by reality, every movement in life became more difficult for the dreamer, for Paul, his fear of errors being like the opium dreamer's fear of noise or daylight.

And not only his dream of Djuna was he seeking to

preserve like some fragile essence easily dispelled but even more dangerous, his own image of what was expected of him by Djuna, what he imagined Djuna expected of him—a heavy demand upon a youthful Paul, his own ideal exigencies which he did not know to be invented by himself creating a difficulty in every act or word in which he was merely re-enacting scenes rehearsed in childhood in which the child's naturalness was always defeated by the severity of the parents giving him the perpetual feeling that no word and no act came up to this impossible standard set for him. A more terrible compression than when the Chinese bound the feet of their infants, bound them with yards of cloth to stunt the natural growth. Such tyrannical cloth worn too long, unbroken, uncut, would in the end turn one into a mummy. . . .

Djuna could see the image of the mother binding Paul in the story he told her: He had a pet guinea pig, once, which he loved. And his mother had forced him to kill it.

She could see all the bindings when he added: "I destroyed a diary I kept in school."

"Why?"

"Now that I was home for a month, my parents might have read it."

Were the punishments so great that he was willing rather to annihilate living parts of himself, a loved pet, a diary reflecting his inner self?

"There are many sides of yourself you cannot show your parents."

"Yes." An expression of anxiety came to his face. The effect of their severity was apparent in the way he sat, stood—even in the tone of resignation in which he said: "I have to leave soon."

Djuna looked at him and saw him as the prisoner he was—a prisoner of school, of parents.

"But you have a whole month of freedom now."

"Yes," said Paul, but the word freedom had no echo in his being.

"What will you do with it?"

He smiled then. "I can't do much with it. My parents don't want me to visit dancers."

"Did you tell them you were coming to visit me?"

"Yes."

"Do they know you want to be a dancer yourself?"

"Oh, no." He smiled again, a distressed smile, and then his eyes lost their direct, open frankness. They wavered, as if he had suddenly lost his way.

This was his most familiar expression: a nebulous glance, sliding off people and objects.

He had the fears of a child in the external world, yet he gave at the same time the impression of living in a larger world. This boy, thought Djuna tenderly, is lost. But he is lost in a large world. His dreams are vague, infinite, formless. He loses himself in them. No one knows what he is imagining and thinking. He does not know, he cannot say, but it is not a simple world. It expands beyond his grasp, he senses more than he knows, a bigger world which frightens him. He cannot confide or give himself. He must have been too often harshly condemned.

Waves of tenderness flowed out to him from her eyes as they sat without talking. The cloud vanished from his face. It was as if he sensed what she was thinking.

Just as he was leaving Lawrence arrived breathlessly, embraced Djuna effusively, pranced into the studio and turned on the radio.

He was Paul's age, but unlike Paul he did not appear to carry a little snail house around his personality, a place into which to retreat and vanish. He came out openly, eyes aware, smiling, expectant, in readiness for anything that might happen. He moved propelled by sheer impulse, and was never still.

He was carrying a cage which he laid in the middle of the room. He lifted its covering shaped like a miniature striped awning.

59

Djuna knelt on the rug to examine the contents of the cage and laughed to see a blue mouse nibbling at a cracker.

"Where did you find a turquoise mouse?" asked Djuna.

"I bathed her in dye," said Lawrence. "Only she licks it all away in a few days and turns white again, so I had to bring her this time right after her bath."

The blue mouse was nibbling eagerly. The music was playing. They were sitting on the rug. The room began to glitter and sparkle.

Paul looked on with amazement.

(This pet, his eyes said, need not be killed. Nothing is forbidden here.)

Lawrence was painting the cage with phosphorescent paint so that it would shine in the dark.

"That way she won't be afraid when I leave her alone at night!"

While the paint dried Lawrence began to dance.

Djuna was laughing behind her veil of long hair.

Paul looked at them yearningly and then said in a toneless voice: "I have to leave now." And he left precipitately.

"Who is the beautiful boy?" asked Lawrence.

"The son of tyrannical parents who are very worried he should visit a dancer."

"Will he come again?"

"He made no promise. Only if he can get away."

"We'll go and visit him."

Djuna smiled. She could imagine Lawrence arriving at Paul's formal home with a cage with a blue mouse in it and Paul's mother saying: "You get rid of that pet!"

Or Lawrence taking a ballet leap to touch the tip of a chandelier, or singing some delicate obscenity.

"*C'est une jeune fille en fleur,*" he said now, clairvoyantly divining Djuna's fear of never escaping from the echoes and descendants of Michael.

Lawrence shrugged his shoulders. Then he looked at her with his red-gold eyes, under his red-gold hair. Whenever he looked at her it was contagious: that eager, ardent glance falling amorously on everyone and everything, dissolving the darkest moods.

No sadness could resist this frenzied carnival of affection he dispensed every day, beginning with his enthusiasm for his first cup of coffee, joy at the day's beginning, an immediate fancy for the first person he saw, a passion at the least provocation for man, woman, child or animal. A warmth even in his collisions with misfortunes, troubles and difficulties.

He received them smiling. Without money in his pocket he rushed to help. With generous excess he rushed to love, to desire, to possess, to lose, to suffer, to die the multiple little deaths everyone dies each day. He would even die and weep and suffer and lose with enthusiasm, with ardor. He was prodigal in poverty, rich and abundant in some invisible chemical equivalent to gold and sun.

Any event would send him leaping and prancing with gusto: a concert, a play, a ballet, a person. Yes, yes, yes, cried his young firm body every morning. No retractions, no hesitations, no fears, no caution, no economy. He accepted every invitation.

His joy was in movement, in assenting, in consenting, in expansion.

Whenever he came he lured Djuna into a swirl. Even in sadness they smiled at each other, expanding in sadness with dilated eyes and dilated hearts.

"Drop every sorrow and dance!"

Thus they healed each other by dancing, perfectly mated in enthusiasm and fire.

The waves which carried him forward never dropped him on the rocks. He would always come back smiling: "Oh, Djuna, you remember Hilda? I was so crazy about her. Do you know what she did? She tried to palm off some false money on me. Yes, with all her lovely eyes, manners, sensitiveness, she came to me and said so ten-

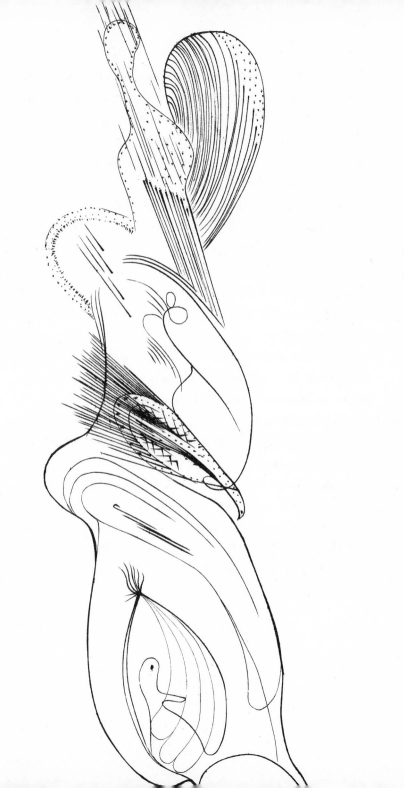

derly: let me have change for this ten-dollar bill. And it was a bad one. And then she tried to hide some drugs in my room, and to say I was the culprit. I nearly went to jail. She pawned my typewriter, my box of paints. She finally took over my room and I had to sleep for the night on a park bench."

But the next morning he was again full of faith, love, trust, impulses.

Dancing and believing.

In his presence she was again ready to believe.

To believe in Paul's eyes, the mystery and the depth in them, the sense of some vast dream lying coiled there, undeciphered.

Lawrence had finished the phosphorescent painting. He closed the curtains and the cage shone in the dark. Now he decided to paint with phosphorescence everything paintable in the room.

The next day Lawrence appeared with a large pot of paint and he was stirring it with a stick when Paul telephoned: "I can get away for a while. May I come?"

"Oh, come, come," said Djuna.

"I can't stay very late. . . ." His voice was muffled, like that of a sick person. There was a plaintiveness in it so plainly audible to Djuna's heart.

"The prisoner is allowed an hour's freedom," she said.

When Paul came Lawrence handed him a paintbrush and in silence the two of them worked at touching up everything paintable in the room. They turned off the lights. A new room appeared.

Luminous faces appeared on the walls, new flowers, new jewels, new castles, new jungles, new animals, all in filaments of light.

Mysterious translucence like their unmeasured words, their impulsive acts, wishes, enthusiasms. Darkness was excluded from their world, the darkness of loss of faith. It was now the room with a perpetual sparkle, even in darkness.

(They are making a new world for me, felt Djuna, a world of greater lightness. It is perhaps a dream and I may not be allowed to stay. They treat me as one of their own, because I believe what they believe, I feel as they do. I hate the father, authority, men of power, men of wealth, all tyranny, all authority, all crystallizations. I feel as Lawrence and Paul: outside there lies a bigger world full of cruelties, dangers and corruptions, where one sells out one's charms, one's playfulness, and enters a rigid world of discipline, duty, contracts, accountings. A thick opaque world without phosphorescence. I want to stay in this room forever not with man the father but with man the son, carving, painting, dancing, dreaming, and always beginning, born anew every day, never aging, full of faith and impulse, turning and changing to every wind like the mobiles. I do not love those who have ceased to flow, to believe, to feel. Those who can no longer melt, exult, who cannot let themselves be cheated, laugh at loss, those who are bound and frozen.)

She laid her head on Lawrence's shoulder with a kind of gratitude.

(Nowhere else as here with Lawrence and with Paul was there such an iridescence in the air; nowhere else so far from the threat of hardening and crystallizing. Everything flowing. . . .)

Djuna was brushing her hair with her fingers, in long pensive strokes, and Lawrence was talking about the recurrent big problem of a job. He had tried so many. How to work without losing one's color, one's ardor, personal possessions and freedom. He was very much like a delicate Egyptian scarab who dreaded to lose his iridescence in routine, in duty, in monotony. The job could kill one, or maim one, make one a robot, an opaque personage, a future undertaker, a man of power with gouty limbs and a hardening of the arteries of faith!

Lawrence was now working in a place which made decorations for shop windows. He liked to work at night, to go on strange expeditions in the company of mannequins, papier-mâché horses, to live on miniature stages building jungles, sea landscapes, fabulous animals. To flirt with naked mannequins whose arms came off as easily as other women's gloves, who deposited their heads on the floor and took off their wigs when they took off their hats. He became an expert at dismantling women!

Lawrence lived and breathed color and there was no danger of his dying of drabness, for even accidents took on a most vivid shade and a spilled pot of *gouache* was still a delight to the eyes.

He brought Djuna gifts of chokers, headdresses, earrings made of painted clay which crumbled quickly like the trappings for a costume play.

She had always liked objects without solidity. The solid ones bound her to permanency. She had never wanted a solid house, enduring furniture. All these were traps. Then you belonged to them forever. She preferred stage trappings which she could move into and out of easily, without regret. Soon after they fell apart and nothing was lost. The vividness alone survived.

She remembered once hearing a woman complain that armchairs no longer lasted twenty years, and Djuna answered: "But I couldn't love an armchair for twenty years!"

And so change, mutations like the rainbow, and she preferred Lawrence's gifts from which the colored powder and crystals fell like the colors on the wings of butterflies after yielding their maximum of charm.

Paul was carving a piece of copper, making such fine incisions with the scissors that the bird which finally appeared between his slender fingers bristled with filament feathers.

He stood on the table and hung it by a thread to the ceiling. The slightest breath caused it to turn slowly.

Paul had the skin of a child that had never been touched by anything of this earth: no soap, no washrag, no brush, no human kiss could have touched his skin! Never scrubbed, rubbed, scratched, or wrinkled by a pillow. The transparency of the child skin, of the adolescent later to turn opaque. What do children nourish themselves with that their skin has this transparency, and what do they eat of later which brings on opaqueness?

The mothers who kiss them are eating light.

There is a phosphorescence which comes from the magic world of childhood.

Where does this illumination go later? Is it the substance of faith which shines from their bodies like phosphorescence from the albatross, and what kills it?

Now Lawrence had discovered a coiled measuring tape of steel in Djuna's closet while delving for objects useful for charades.

When entirely pulled out of its snail covering it stretched like a long snake of steel which under certain manipulations could stand rigid like a sword or undulate like silver-tipped waves, or flash like lightning.

Lawrence and Paul stood like expert swordsmen facing each other for a duel of light and steel.

The steel band flexed, then hardened between them like a bridge, and at each forward movement by one it seemed as if the sword had pierced the body of the other.

At other moments it wilted, wavered like a frightened snake, and then it looked bedraggled and absurd and they both laughed.

But soon they learned never to let it break or waver and it became like a thunderbolt in their hands. Paul attacked with audacity and Lawrence parried with swiftness.

At midnight Paul began to look anxious. His luminosity clouded, he resumed his hesitant manner. He ceased to occupy the center of the room and moved out of the focus of light and laughter. Like a sleepwalker, he moved away from gaiety.

Djuna walked with him towards the door. They were alone and then he said: "My parents have forbidden me to come here."

"But you were happy here, weren't you?"

"Yes, I was happy."

"This is where you belong."

"Why do you think I belong here?"

"You're gifted for dancing, for painting, for writing. And this is your month of freedom."

"Yes, I know. I wish . . . I wish I were free. . . ."

"If you wish it deeply enough you will find a way."

"I would like to run away, but I have no money."

"If you run away we'll all take care of you."

"Why?"

"Because we believe in you, because you're worth helping."

"I have nowhere to go."

"We'll find you a room somewhere, and we will adopt you. And you will have your month of life."

"Of life!" he repeated with docility.

"But I don't want you to do it unless you feel ready, unless you want it so much that you're willing to sacrifice everything else. I only want you to know you can count on us, but it must be your decision, or it will not mean anything."

"Thank you." This time he did not clasp her hand, he laid his hand within hers as if nestling it there, folded, ivory smooth and gentle, at rest, in an act of trustingness.

Then before leaving the place he looked once more at the room as if to retain its enfolding warmth. At one moment he had laughed so much that he had slid from his chair. Djuna had made him laugh. At that moment many of his chains must have broken, for nothing breaks chains like laughter, and Djuna could not remember in all her life a greater joy than this spectacle of Paul laughing like a released prisoner.

Two days later Paul appeared at her door with his valise.

Djuna received him gaily as if this were the beginning of a holiday, asked him to tie the velvet bows at her wrist, drove him to where Lawrence lived with his parents and where there was an extra room.

She would have liked to shelter him in her own house, but she knew his parents would come there and find him.

He wrote a letter to his parents. He reminded them that he had only a month of freedom for himself before leaving for India on the official post his father had arranged for him, that during this month he felt he had a right to be with whatever friends he felt a kinship with. He had found people with whom he had a great deal to share and since his parents had been so extreme in their demands, forbidding him to see his friends at all, he was being equally extreme in his assertion of his freedom. Not to be concerned about him, that at the end of the month he would comply with his father's plans for him.

He did not stay in his room. It had been arranged that he would have his meals at Djuna's house. An hour after he had laid down his valise in Lawrence's room he was at her house.

In his presence she did not feel herself a mature woman, but again a girl of seventeen at the beginning of her own life. As if the girl of seventeen had remained undestroyed by experience—like some deeper layer in a geological structure which had been pressed but not obliterated by the new layers.

(He seems hungry and thirsty for warmth, and yet so fearful. We are arrested by each other's elusiveness. Who will take flight first? If we move too hastily fear will spring up and separate us. I am fearful of his innocence, and he of what he believes to be my knowingness.

But neither one of us knows what the other wants, we are both arrested and ready to vanish, with such a fear of being hurt. His oscillations are like mine, his muteness like mine at his age, his fears like my fears.)

She felt that as she came nearer there was a vibration through his body. Through all the mists as her body approached to greet him there was an echo of her movements within him.

With his hand within hers, at rest, he said: "Everyone is doing so much for me. Do you think that when I grow up I will be able to do the same for someone else?"

"Of course you will." And because he had said so gently "when I grow up" she saw him suddenly as a boy, and her hand went out swiftly towards the strand of boyish hair which fell over his eyes and pulled it.

That she had done this with a half-frightened laugh as if she expected retaliation made him feel at ease with her.

He did retaliate by trying jiujitsu on her arm until she said: "You hurt me." Then he stopped, but the discovery that her bones were not as strong as the boys' on whom he had tested his knowledge made him feel powerful. He had more strength than he needed to handle her. He could hurt her so easily, and now he was no longer afraid when her face came near his and her eyes grew larger and more brilliant, or when she danced and her hair accidentally swung across her face like a silk whip, or when she sat like an Arab holding conversation over the telephone in answer to invitations which might deprive him of her presence. No matter who called, she always refused, and stayed at home to talk with him.

The light in the room became intensely bright and they were bathed in it, bright with the disappearance of his fear.

He felt at ease to sit and draw, to read, to paint, and to be silent. The light around them grew warm and dim and intimate.

By shedding in his presence the ten years of life which created distance between them, she felt herself re-entering a smaller house of innocence and faith, and that what she shed was merely a role: she had played a role of woman, and this had been the torment, she had been pretending to be a woman, and now she knew she had not been at ease in this role, and now with Paul she felt she was being transformed into a stature and substance nearer to her true state.

With Paul she was passing from an insincere pretense at maturity into a more vulnerable world, escaping from the more difficult role of tormented woman to a smaller room of warmth.

For one moment, sitting there with Paul, listening to the Symphony in D minor of César Franck, through his eyes she was allowed behind the mirror into a smaller silk-lined house of faith.

In art, in history man fights his fears, he wants to live forever, he is afraid of death, he wants to work with other men, he wants to live forever. He is like a child afraid of death. The child is afraid of death, of darkness, of solitude. Such simple fears behind all the elaborate constructions. Such simple fears as hunger for light, warmth, love. Such simple fears behind the elaborate constructions of art. Examine them all gently and quietly through the eyes of a boy. There is always a human being lonely, a human being afraid, a human being lost, a human being confused. Concealing and disguising his dependence, his needs, ashamed to say: I am a simple human being in too vast and too complex a world. Because of all we have discovered about a leaf. . . it is still a leaf. Can we relate to a leaf, on a tree, in a park, a simple leaf: green, glistening, sun-bathed or wet, or turning white because the storm is coming. Like the savage, let us look at the leaf wet or shining with sun, or white with fear of the storm, or silvery in the fog, or listless in too great heat, or falling in the autumn, drying, reborn each year anew. Learn from the leaf: simplicity. In spite of all we know about the leaf: its nerve structure phyllome cellular papilla parenchyma stomata venation. Keep a human relation—leaf, man, woman, child. In tenderness. No matter how immense the world, how elaborate, how contradictory, there is always man, woman, child, and the leaf. Humanity makes everything warm and simple. Humanity. Let the waters of humanity flow through the abstract city, through abstract art, weeping like rivulets cracking rocky mountains, melting icebergs. The frozen worlds in empty cages of mobiles where hearts lie exposed like wires in an electric bulb. Let them burst at the tender touch of a leaf.

The next morning Djuna was having breakfast in bed when Lawrence appeared.

"I'm broke and I'd like to have breakfast with you."

He had begun to eat his toast when the maid came and said: "There's a gentleman at the door who won't give his name."

"Find out what he wants. I don't want to dress yet."

But the visitor had followed the servant to the door and stood now in the bedroom.

Before anyone could utter a protest he said in the most classically villainous tone: "Ha, ha, having breakfast, eh?"

"Who are you? What right have you to come in here," said Djuna.

"I have every right: I'm a detective."

"A detective!"

Lawrence's eyes began to sparkle with amusement.

The detective said to him: "And what are you doing here, young man?"

"I'm having breakfast." He said this in the most cheerful and natural manner, continuing to drink his coffee and buttering a piece of toast which he offered Djuna.

"Wonderful!" said the detective. "So I've caught you. Having breakfast, eh? While your parents are breaking their hearts over your disappearance. Having breakfast, eh? When you're not eighteen yet and they can force you to return home and never let you out again." And turning to Djuna he added: "And what may your interest in this young man be?"

Then Djuna and Lawrence broke into irrepressible laughter.

"I'm not the only one," said Lawrence.

At this the detective looked like a man who had not expected his task to be so easy, almost grateful for the collaboration.

"So you're not the only one!"

Djuna stopped laughing. "He means anyone who is broke can have breakfast here."

"Will you have a cup of coffee?" said Lawrence with an impudent smile.

"That's enough talk from you," said the detective. "You'd better come along with me, Paul."

"But I'm not Paul."

"Who are you?"

"My name is Lawrence."

"Do you know Paul—? Have you seen him recently?"

"He was here last night for a party."

"A party? And where did he go after that?"

"I don't know," said Lawrence. "I thought he was staying with his parents."

"What kind of a party was this?" asked the detective.

But now Djuna had stopped laughing and was becoming angry. "Leave this place immediately," she said.

The detective took a photograph out of his pocket, compared it with Lawrence's face, saw there was no resemblance, looked once more at Djuna's face, read the anger in it, and left.

As soon as he left her anger vanished and they laughed again. Suddenly Djuna's playfulness turned into anxiety. "But this may become serious. Lawrence. Paul won't be able to come to my house any more. And suppose it had been Paul who had come for breakfast!"

And then another aspect of the situation struck her and her face became sorrowful. "What kind of parents has Paul that they can consider using force to bring him home."

She took up the telephone and called Paul. Paul said in a shocked voice: "They can't take me home by force!"

"I don't know about the law, Paul. You'd better stay away from my house. I will meet you somewhere—say at the ballet theater—until we find out."

For a few days they met at concerts, galleries, ballets. But no one seemed to follow them.

Djuna lived in constant fear that he would be whisked away and that she might never see him again. Their meetings took on the anxiety of repeated farewells. They always looked at each other as if it were for the last time.

Through this fear of loss she took longer glances at his face, and every facet of it, every gesture, every inflection of his voice thus sank deeper into her, to be stored away against future loss—deeper and deeper it penetrated, impregnated her more as she fought against its vanishing.

She felt that she not only saw Paul vividly in the present but Paul in the future. Every expression she could read as an indication of future power, future discernment, future completion. Her vision of the future Paul illumined the present. Others could see a young man experiencing his first drunkenness, taking his first steps in the world, oscillating or contradicting himself. But she felt herself living with a Paul no one had seen yet, the man of the future, willful, and with a power in him which appeared intermittently.

When the clouds and mists of adolescence would vanish, what a complete and rich man he would become, with this mixture of sensibility and intelligence motivating his choices, discarding shallowness, never taking a step into mediocrity, with an unerring instinct for the extraordinary.

To send a detective to bring him home by force, how little his parents must know this Paul of the future, possessed of that deep-seated mine of tenderness hidden below access but visible to her.

She was living with a Paul no one knew as yet, in a

secret relationship far from the reach of the subtlest detectives, beyond the reach of the entire world.

Under the veiled voice she felt the hidden warmth, under the hesitancies a hidden strength, under the fears a vaster dream more difficult to size and to fulfill.

Alone, after an afternoon with him, she lay on her bed and while the bird he had carved gyrated lightly in the center of the room, tears came to her eyes so slowly she did not feel them at first until they slid down her cheeks.

Tears from this unbearable melting of her heart and body—a complete melting before the face of Paul, and the muted way his body spoke, the gentle way he was hungering, reaching, groping, like a prisoner escaping slowly and gradually, door by door, room by room, hallway by hallway, towards the light. The prison that had been built around him had been of darkness: darkness about himself, about his needs, about his true nature.

The solitary cell created by the parents.

He knew nothing, nothing about his true self. And such blindness was as good as binding him with chains. His parents and his teachers had merely imposed upon him a false self that seemed right to them.

This boy they did not know.

But this melting, it must not be. She turned her face away, to the right now, as if to turn away from the vision of his face, and murmured: "I must not love him, I must not love him."

The bell rang. Before she could sit up Paul had come in.

"Oh, Paul, this is dangerous for you!"

"I had to come."

As he stopped in his walking towards her his body sought to convey a message. What was his body saying? What were his eyes saying?

He was too near, she felt his eyes possessing her and she rushed away to make tea, to place a tray and food between them, like some very fragile wall made of sand, in games of childhood, which the sea could so easily wash away!

She talked, but he was not listening, nor was she listening to her own words, for his smile penetrated her, and she wanted to run away from him.

"I would like to know . . ." he said, and the words remained suspended.

He sat too near. She felt the unbearable melting, the loss of herself, and she struggled to close some door against him. "I must not love him, I must not love him!"

She moved slightly away, but his hair was so near her hand that her fingers were drawn magnetically to touch it lightly, playfully.

"What do you want to know?"

Had he noticed her own trembling? He did not answer her. He leaned over swiftly and took her whole mouth in his, the whole man in him coming out in a direct thrust, firm, willful, hungry. With one kiss he appropriated her, asserted his possessiveness.

When he had taken her mouth and kissed her until they were both breathless they lay side by side and she felt his body strong and warm against hers, his passion inflexible.

He laid his hand over her with hesitations. Everything was new to him, a woman's neck, a shoulder, a woman's hooks and buttons.

Between the journeys of discovery he had flickering instants of uncertainties until the sparks of pleasure guided his hand.

Where he passed his hand no one else had ever passed his hand. New cells awakened under his delicate fingers never wakened before to say: this is yours.

A breast touched for the first time is a breast never touched before.

He looked at her with his long blue eyes which had

never wept and her eyes were washed luminous and clear, her eyes forgot they had wept.

He touched her eyelashes with his eyelashes of which not one had fallen out and those of hers which had been washed away by tears were replaced.

His hair which had never been crushed between feverish pillows, knotted by nightmares, mingled with hers and untangled it.

Where sadness had carved rich caverns he sank his youthful thrusts grasping endless sources of warmth.

Only before the last mystery of the body did he pause. He had thrust and entered and now he paused.

Did one lie still and at peace in the secret place of woman?

In utter silence they lay.

Fever mounting in him, the sap rising, the bodies taut with a need of violence.

She made one undulatory movement, and this unlocked in him a whirlpool of desire, a dervish dance of all the silver knives of pleasure.

When they awakened from their trance, they smiled at each other, but he did not move. They lay merged, slimness to slimness, legs like twin legs, hip to hip.

The cotton of silence lay all around them, covering their bodies in quilted softness.

The big wave of fire which rolled them washed them ashore tenderly into small circles of foam.

On the table there was a huge vase filled with tulips. She moved towards them, seeking something to touch, to pour her joy into, out of the exaltation she felt.

Every part of her body that had been opened by his hands yearned to open the whole world in harmony with her mood.

She looked at the tulips so hermetically closed, like secret poems, like the secrets of the flesh. Her hands took each tulip, the ordinary tulip of everyday living and she slowly opened them, petal by petal, opened them tenderly.

They were changed from plain to exotic flowers, from closed secrets to open flowering.

Then she heard Paul say: "Don't do that!"

There was a great anxiety in his voice. He repeated: "Don't do that!"

She felt a great stab of anxiety. Why was he so disturbed?

She looked at the flowers. She looked at Paul's face lying on the pillow, clouded with anxiety, and she was struck with fear. Too soon. She had opened him to love too soon. He was not ready.

Even with tenderness, even with delicate fingers, even with the greatest love, it had been too soon! She had forced time, as she had forced the flowers to change from the ordinary to the extraordinary. He was not ready!

Now she understood her own hesitations, her impulse to run away from him. Even though he had made the first gesture, she, knowing, should have saved him from anxiety.

(Paul was looking at the opened tulips and seeing in them something else, not himself but Djuna, the opening body of Djuna. Don't let her open the flowers as he had opened her. In the enormous wave of silence, the hypnosis of hands, skin, delight, he had heard a small moan, yet in her face he had seen joy. Could the thrust into her have hurt her? It was like stabbing someone, this desire.)

"I'm going to dress, now," she said lightly. She could not close the tulips again, but she could dress. She could close herself again and allow him to close again.

Watching her he felt a violent surge of strength again, stronger than his fears. "Don't dress yet."

Again he saw on her face a smile he had never seen there in her gayest moments, and then he accepted the mystery and abandoned himself to his own joy.

His heart beat wildly at her side, wildly in panic and

joy together at the moment before taking her. This wildly beating heart at her side, beating against hers, and then the cadenced, undulating, blinding merging together, and no break between their bodies afterwards.

After the storm he lay absolutely still over her body, dreaming, quiet, as if this were the place of haven. He lay given, lost, entranced. She bore his weight with joy, though after a while it numbed and hurt her. She made a slight movement, and then he asked her: "Am I crushing you?"

"You're flattening me into a thin wafer," she said, smiling, and he smiled back, then laughed.

"The better to eat you, my dear."

He kissed her again as if he would eat her with delight.

Then he got up and made a somersault on the carpet, with light exultant gestures.

She lay back watching the copper bird gyrating in the center of the room.

His gaiety suddenly overflowed, and taking a joyous leap in the air, he came back to her and said:

"I will call up my father!"

She could not understand. He leaned over her body and keeping his hand over her breast he dialed his father's telephone number.

Then she could see on his face what he wanted to tell his father: call his father, tell him what could not be told, but which his entire new body wanted to tell him: I have taken a woman! I have a woman of my own. I am your equal, Father! I am a man!

When his father answered Paul could only say the ordinary words a son can say to his father, but he uttered these ordinary words with exultant arrogance, as if his father could see him with his hand on Djuna's body: "Father, I am here."

"Where are you?" answered the father severely. "We're expecting you home. You can continue to see your friends but you must come home to please your mother. Your mother has dinner all ready for you!"

Paul laughed, laughed as he had never laughed as a boy, with his hand over the mouth of the telephone.

On such a day they are expecting him for dinner!

They were blind to the miracle. Over the telephone his father should hear and see that he had a woman of his own: she was lying there smiling.

How dare the father command now, doesn't he hear the new voice of the new man in his son?

He hung up.

His hair was falling over his eager eyes. Djuna pulled

at it. He stopped her. "You can't do that any more, oh, no." And he sank his teeth into the softest part of her neck.

"You're sharpening your teeth to become a great lover," she said.

When desire overtook him he always had a moment of wildly beating heart, almost of distress, before the invading tide. Before closing his eyes to kiss her, before abandoning himself, he always carefully closed the shutters, windows and doors.

This was the secret act, and he feared the eyes of the world upon him. The world was full of eyes upon his acts, eyes watching with disapproval.

That was the secret fear left from his childhood: dreams, wishes, acts, pleasures which aroused condemnation in the parents' eyes. He could not remember one glance of approval, of love, of admiration, of consent. From far back he remembered being driven into secrecy because whatever he revealed seemed to arouse disapproval or punishment.

He had read the *Arabian Nights* in secret, he had smoked in secret, he had dreamed in secret.

His parents had questioned him only to accuse him later.

And so he closed the shutters, curtains, windows, and then went to her and both of them closed their eyes upon their caresses.

There was a knitted blanket over the couch which he particularly liked. He would sit under it as if it were a tent. Through the interstices of the knitting he could see her and the room as through an oriental trellis. With one hand out of the blanket he would seek her little finger with his little finger and hold it.

As in an opium dream, this touching and interlacing of two little fingers became an immense gesture, the very fragile bridge of their relationship. By this little finger so gently and so lightly pulling hers he took her whole self as no one else had.

He drew her under the blanket thus, in a dreamlike way, by a small gesture containing the greatest power, a greater power than violence.

Once there they both felt secure from all the world, and from all threats, from the father and the detective, and all the taboos erected to separate lovers all over the world.

Lawrence rushed over to warn them that Paul's father had been seen driving through the neighborhood.

Paul and Djuna were having dinner together and were going to the ballet.

Paul had painted a feather bird for Djuna's hair and she was pinning it on when Lawrence came with the warning.

Paul became a little pale, then smiled and said: "Wafer, in case my father comes, could you make yourself less pretty?"

Djuna went and washed her face of all make-up, and then she unpinned the airy feather bird from her hair, and they sat down together to wait for the father.

Djuna said: "I'm going to tell you the story of Caspar Hauser, which is said to have happened many years ago in Austria. Caspar Hauser was about seventeen years old when he appeared in the city, a wanderer, lost and bewildered. He had been imprisoned in a dark room since childhood. His real origin was unknown, and the cause for the imprisonment. It was believed to be a court intrigue, that he might have been put away to substitute another ruler, or that he might have been an illegitimate son of the Queen. His jailer died and the boy found himself free. In solitude he had grown into manhood with the spirit of a child. He had only one dream in his possession, which he looked upon as a memory. He had once lived in a castle. He had been led to a room to see his mother. His mother stood behind a door. But he had never reached her. Was it a dream or a memory? He wanted to find this castle again, and his mother. The people of the city adopted him as a curiosity. His honesty, his immediate, childlike instinct about people, both infuriated and interested them. They tampered with him. They wanted to impose their beliefs on him, teach him, possess him. But the boy could sense their falsities, their treacheries, their self-interest. He belonged to his dream. He gave his whole faith only to the man who promised to take him back to his home and to his mother. And this man betrayed him, delivered him to his enemies. Just before his death he had met a woman, who had not dared to love him because he was so young, who had stifled her feeling. If she had dared he might have escaped his fate."

"Why didn't she dare?" asked Paul.

"She saw only the obstacle," said Djuna. "Most people see only the obstacle, and are stopped by it."

(No harm can befall you now, Paul, no harm can befall you. You have been set free. You made a good beginning. You were loved by the first object of your desire. Your first desire was answered. I made such a bad beginning! I began with a closed door. This harmed me, but you at least began with fulfillment. You were not hurt. You were not denied. I am the only one in danger. For that is all I am allowed to give you, a good beginning, and then I must surrender you.)

They sat and waited for the father.

Lawrence left them. The suspense made him uneasy.

Paul was teaching Djuna how to eat rice with chopsticks. Then he carefully cleaned them and was holding them now as they talked as if they were puppets representing a Balinese shadow theater of the thoughts neither one dared to formulate.

They sat and waited for the father.

Paul was holding the chopsticks like impudent puppets, gesticulating, then he playfully unfastened the first button of her blouse with them, deftly, and they laughed together.

"It's time for the ballet," said Djuna. "Your father is evidently not coming, or he would be here already."

She saw the illumination of desire light his face.

"Wait, Djuna." He unfastened the second button, and the third.

Then he laid his head on her breast and said: "Let's not go anywhere tonight, let's stay here."

Paul despised small and shallow waves. He was drawn to a vastness which corresponded to his boundless dreams. He must possess the world in some big way, rule a large kingdom, expand in some absolute leadership.

He felt himself a king as a child feels king, over kingdoms uncharted by ordinary men. He would not have the ordinary, the known. Only the vast, the unknown could satisfy him.

Djuna was a woman with echoes plunging into an endless past he could never explore completely. When he tasted her he tasted a suffering which had borne a fragrance, a fragrance which made deeper grooves. It was enough that he sensed the dark forests of experience, the unnamed rivers, the enigmatic mountains, the rich mines under the ground, the overflowing caves of secret knowledges. A vast ground for an intrepid adventurer.

Above all she was his "ocean" as he wrote her. "When a man takes a woman to himself he possesses the sea."

The waves, the enormous waves of a woman's love!

She was a sea whose passions could rise sometimes into larger waves than he felt capable of facing!

Much as he loved danger, the unknown, the vast, he felt too the need of taking flight, to put distance and space between himself and the ocean for fear of being submerged!

Flight: into silence, into a kind of invisibility by

which he could be sitting there on the floor while yet creating an impression of absence, able to disappear into a book, a drawing, into the music he listened to.

She was gazing at his little finger and the extreme fragility and sensitiveness of it astonished her.

(He is the transparent child.)

Before this transparent finger so artfully carved, sensitively wrought, boned, which alighted on objects with a touch of air and magic, at the marvel of it, the ephemeral quality of it, a wave of passion would mount within her and exactly like the wave of the ocean intending merely to roll over, cover the swimmer with an explosion of foam, in a rhythm of encompassing, and withdrawing, without intent to drag him to the bottom.

But Paul, with the instinct of the new swimmer, felt that there were times when he could securely hurl himself into the concave heart of the wave and be lifted into ecstasy and be delivered back again on the shore safe and whole; but that there were other times when this great inward curve disguised an undertow, times when he measured his strength and found it insufficient to return to shore.

Then he took up again the lighter games of his recently surrendered childhood.

Djuna found him gravely bending over a drawing

and it was not what he did which conveyed his remoteness, but his way of sitting hermetically closed like some secret Chinese box whose surface showed no possibility of opening.

He sat then as children do, immured in his particular lonely world then, having built a magnetic wall of detachment.

It was then that he practiced as deftly as older men the great objectivity, the long-range view by which men eluded all personal difficulties: he removed himself from the present and the personal by entering into the most abstruse intricacies of a chess game, by explaining to her what Darwin had written when comparing the eye to a microscope, by dissertating on the pleuronectidae or flat fish, so remarkable for their asymmetrical bodies.

And Djuna followed this safari into the worlds of science, chemistry, geology with an awkwardness which was not due to any laziness of mind, but to the fact that the large wave of passion which had been roused in her at the prolonged sight of Paul's little finger was so difficult to dam, because the feeling of wonder before this spectacle was to her as great as that of the explorers before a new mountain peak, of the scientists before a new discovery.

She knew what excitement enfevered men at such

moments of their lives, but she did not see any difference between the beauty of a high flight above the clouds and the subtly colored and changing landscape of adolescence she traversed through the contemplation of Paul's little finger.

A study of anthropological excavations made in Peru was no more wonderful to her than the half-formed dreams unearthed with patience from Paul's vague words, dreams of which they were only catching the prologue; and no forest of precious woods could be more varied than the oscillations of his extreme vulnerability which forced him to take cover, to disguise his feelings, to swing so movingly between great courage and a secret fear of pain.

The birth of his awareness was to her no lesser miracle than the discoveries of chemistry, the variations in his temperature, the mysterious angers, the sudden serenities, no less valuable than the studies of remote climates.

But when in the face of too large a wave, whose dome seemed more than a mere ecstasy of foam raining over the marvelous shape of his hands, a wave whose concaveness seemed more than a temporary womb in which he could lie for the fraction of an instant, the duration of an orgasm, he sat like a Chinese secret box with a surface revealing no possible opening to the infiltrations of tenderness or the flood of passion, then her larger impulse fractured with a strange pain into a multitude of little waves capped with frivolous sun-spangles, secretly ashamed of its wild disproportion to the young man who sat there offering whatever he possessed—his intermittent manliness, his vastest dreams and his fear of his own expansions, his maturity as well as his fear of this maturity which was leading him out of the gardens of childhood.

And when the larger wave had dispersed into smaller ones, and when Paul felt free of any danger of being dragged to the bottom, free of that fear of possession which is the secret of all adolescence, when he had gained strength within his retreat, then he returned to tease and stir her warmth into activity again, when he felt equal to plunging into it, to lose himself in it, feeling the intoxication of the man who had conquered the sea. . . .

Then he would write to her exultantly: you are the sea. . . .

But she could see the little waves in himself gathering power for the future, preparing for the moment when he would be the engulfing one.

Then he seemed no longer the slender adolescent with dreamy gestures but a passionate young man rehearsing his future scenes of domination.

He wore a white scarf through the gray streets of the city, a white scarf of immunity. His head resting on the folds was the head of the dreamer walking through the city selecting by a white magic to see and hear and gather only according to his inner needs, slowly and gradually building as each one does ultimately, his own world out of the material at hand from which he was allowed at least a freedom of selection.

The white scarf asserted the innumerable things which did not touch him: choked trees, broken windows, cripples, obscenities penciled on the walls, the lascivious speeches of the drunks, the miasmas and corrosions of the city.

He did not see or hear them.

After traversing desert streets, immured in his inner dream, he would suddenly open his eyes upon an organ grinder and his monkey.

What he brought home again was always some object by which men sought to overcome mediocrity: a book, a painting, a piece of music to transform his vision of the world, to expand and deepen it.

The white scarf did not lie.

It was the appropriate flag of his voyages.

His head resting fittingly on its white folds was immune to stains. He could traverse sewers, hospitals, prisons, and none left their odor upon him. His coat, his breath, his hair, when he returned, still exhaled the odor of his dream.

This was the only virgin forest known to man: this purity of selection.

When Paul returned with his white scarf gleaming it was all that he rejected which shone in its folds.

He was always a little surprised at older people's interest in him.

He did not know himself to be the possessor of anything they might want, not knowing that in his presence they were violently carried back to their first dream.

Because he stood at the beginning of the labyrinth and not in the heart of it, he made everyone aware of the turn where they had lost themselves. With Paul standing at the entrance of the maze, they recaptured the beginning of their voyage, they remembered their first intent, their first image, their first desires.

They would don his white scarf and begin anew.

And yet today she felt there was another purity, a greater purity which lay in the giving of one's self. She felt pure when she gave herself, and Paul felt pure when he withdrew himself.

The tears of his mother, the more restrained severity of his father, brought him home again.

His eighteenth birthday came and this was the one they could not spend together, this being his birthday in reality, the one visible to his parents. Whereas with Djuna he had spent so many birthdays which his parents could not have observed, with their limited knowledge of him.

They had not attended the birthday of his manhood, the birthday of his roguish humorous self, of his first drunkenness, his first success at a party; or the birthday of his eloquent self on the theme of poetry, painting or music. Or the birthday of his imagination, his fantasy, of his new knowledge of people, of his new assertions and his discoveries of unknown powers in himself.

This succession of birthdays that had taken place since he left home was the highest fiesta ever attended by Djuna, the spectacle of unpredictable blooms, of the shells breaking around his personality, the emergence of the man.

But his real birthday they could not spend together. His mother made dinner for him, and he played chess with his father—they who loved him less and who had bound and stifled him with prohibitions, who had delayed his manhood.

His mother made a birthday cake iced and sprinkled with warnings against expansion, cautions against new friends, designed a border like those of formal gardens as if to outline all the proprieties with which to defeat adventure.

His father played chess with him silently, indicating in the carefully measured moves a judgment upon all the wayward dances of the heart, the caprices of the body, above all a judgment upon such impulses as had contributed to Paul's very presence there, the act of conjunction from which had been formed the luminous boy eating at their table.

The cake they fed him was the cake of caution: to fear all human beings and doubt the motivations of all men and women not listed in the Social Directory.

The candles were not lit to celebrate his future freedom, but to say: only within the radius lighted by these birthday candles, only within the radius of father and mother are you truly safe.

A small circle. And outside of this circle, evil.

And so he ate of this birthday cake baked by his

mother, containing all the philters against love, expansion and freedom known to white voodoo.

A cake to prevent and preserve the child from becoming man!

No more nights together, when to meet the dawn together was the only marriage ceremony accorded to lovers.

But he returned to her one day carrying the valise with his laundry. On his return home he had packed his laundry to have it washed at home. And his mother had said: "Take it back. I won't take care of laundry you soiled while living with strangers."

So quietly he brought it back to Djuna, to the greater love that would gladly take care of his belongings as long as they were the clothes he soiled in his experience with freedom.

The smallness of his shirts hurt her, like a sign of dangers for him which she could not avert. He was still slender enough, young enough to be subjected to tyranny.

They were both listening to César Franck's Symphony in D Minor.

And then the conflicting selves in Djuna fused into one mood as they do at such musical crossroads.

The theme of the symphony was gentleness.

She had first heard it at the age of sixteen one rainy afternoon and associated it with her first experience of love, of a love without climax which she had known with Michael. She had interwoven this music with her first concept of the nature of love as one of ultimate, infinite gentleness.

In César Franck's symphony there was immediate exaltation, dissolution in feeling and the evasion of violence. Over and over again in this musical ascension of emotion, the stairway of fever was climbed and deserted before one reached explosion.

An obsessional return to minor themes, creating an endless tranquillity, and at sixteen she had believed that the experience of love was utterly contained in this gently flowing narcotic, in the delicate spirals, cadences and undulations of this music.

César Franck came bringing messages of softness and trust, accompanying Paul's gestures and attitudes, and for this she trusted him, a passion without the storms of destruction.

She had wanted such nebulous landscapes, such vertiginous spirals without exposions: the drug.

Listening to the symphony flowing and yet not flowing (for there was a static groove in which it remained imprisoned so similar to the walled-in room of her house, containing a mystery of stillness), Djuna saw the Obelisk in the Place de la Concorde, the arrow of stone placed at the center of a gracefully turbulent square, summating gardens, fountains and rivers of automobiles. One pointed dart of stone to pierce the night, the fog, the rain, the sun, aiming faultlessly into the clouds.

And there was the small, crazy woman Matilda, whom everyone knew, who came every morning and sat on one of the benches near the river, and stayed there all day, watching the passers-by, eating sparingly and lightly of some mysterious food in crumbs out of a paper bag, like the pigeons. So familiar to the policeman, to the tourists, and to the permanent inhabitants of the Place de la Concorde, that not to see her there would have been as noticeable, as disturbing, as to find the Obelisk gone, and the square left without its searchlight into the sky.

Matilda was known for her obstinacy in sitting there through winter and summer, her indifference to climate, her vague answers to those who sought her reasons for being there, her tireless watchfulness, as if she were keeping a rendezvous with eternity.

Only at sundown did she leave, sometimes gently incited by the policeman.

Since there was no total deterioration in her clothes,

or in her health, everyone surmised she must have a home and no one was ever concerned about her.

Djuna had once sat beside her and Matilda at first would not speak, but addressed herself to the pigeons and to the falling autumn leaves, murmuring, whispering, muttering by turn. Then suddenly she said to Djuna very simply and clearly: "My lover left me sitting here and said he would come back."

(The policeman had said: I have seen her sitting there for twenty years.)

"How long have you been sitting here and waiting?" Djuna asked.

"I don't know."

She ate of the same bread she was feeding the pigeons. Her face was wrinkled but not aged, through the wrinkles shone an expression which was not of age, which was the expression of alert waiting, watchfulness, expectation of the young.

"He will come back," she said, for the first time a look of defiance washing her face of its spectator's pallor, the pallor of the recluse who lives without intimate relationship to stir the rhythms of the blood, this glazed expression of those who watch the crowd passing by and never recognize a face.

"Of course he will," said Djuna, unable to bear even the shadow of anxiety on the woman's face.

Matilda's face recovered its placidity, its patience.

"He told me to sit here and wait."

A mortal blow had stopped the current of her life, but had not shattered her. It had merely paralyzed her sense of time, she would sit and wait for the lost lover and the years were obliterated by the anesthesia of the deadened cell of time: five minutes stretched to infinity and kept her alive, alive and ghostly, with the cell of time, the little clock of reality inside the brain forever damaged. A faceless clock pointing to anguish. And with time was linked pain, lodged in the same cell (neighbors and twins), time and pain in more or less intimate relationship.

And what was left was this shell of a woman immune to cold and heat, anesthetized by a great loss into immobility and timelessness.

Sitting there beside Matilda Djuna heard the echoes of the broken cell within the little psychic stage of her own heart, so well enacted, so neat, so clear, and wondered whether when her father left the house for good in one of his moods of violence as much damage had been done to her, and whether some part of her being had not been atrophied, preventing complete openness and complete development in living.

By his act of desertion he had destroyed a cell in Djuna's being, an act of treachery from a cruel world setting her against all fathers, while retaining the perilous hope of a father returning under the guise of the men who resembled him, to re-enact again the act of violence.

It was enough for a man to possess certain attributes of the father—any man possessed of power—and then her being came alive with fear as if the entire situation would be re-enacted inevitably: possession, love and desertion, replacing her on a bench like Matilda, awaiting a denouement.

Looking back there had been a momentous break in the flow, a change of activity.

Every authoritarian step announced the return of the father and danger. For the father's last words had been: "I will come back."

Matilda had been more seriously injured: the life flow had stopped. She had retained the first image, the consciousness that she must wait, and the last words spoken by the lover had been a command for eternity: wait until I come back.

As if these words had been uttered by a proficient

hypnotist who had then cut off all her communications with the living, so that she was not permitted even this consolation allowed to other deserted human beings: the capacity to transfer this love to another, to cheat the order given, to resume life with others, to forget the first one.

Matilda had been mercifully arrested and suspended in time, and rendered unconscious of pain.

But not Djuna.

In Djuna the wound had remained alive, and whenever life touched upon this wound she mistook the pain she felt for being alive, and her pain warning her and guiding her to deflect from man the father to man the son.

She could see clearly all the cells of her being, like the rooms of her house which had blossomed, enriched, developed and stretched far and beyond all experiences, but she could see also the cell of her being like the walled-in room of her house in which was lodged violence as having been shut and condemned within her out of fear of disaster.

There was a little cell of her being in which she still existed as a child, which only activated with a subtle anger in the presence of the father, for in relation to him she lost her acquired power, her assurance, she was rendered small again and returned to her former state of helplessness and dependence.

And knowing the tragic outcome of this dependence she felt hostility and her route towards the man of power bristled with this hostility—an immediate need to shut out violence.

Paul and Djuna sat listening to César Franck's, Symphony in D Minor, in this little room of gentleness and trust, barring violence from the world of love, seeking an opiate against destruction and treachery.

So she had allied herself with the son against the father. He had been there to forbid and thus to strengthen the desire. He had been there, large and severe, to threaten the delicate, precarious bond, and thus to render it desperate and make each encounter a reprieve from death and loss.

The movements of the symphony and her movements had been always like Paul's, a ballet of oscillations, peripheral entrances and exits, figures designed to become invisible in moments of danger, pirouetting with all the winged knowledge of birds to avoid collision with violence and severity.

Together they had taken leaps into the air to avoid obstacles.

THE CAFÉ

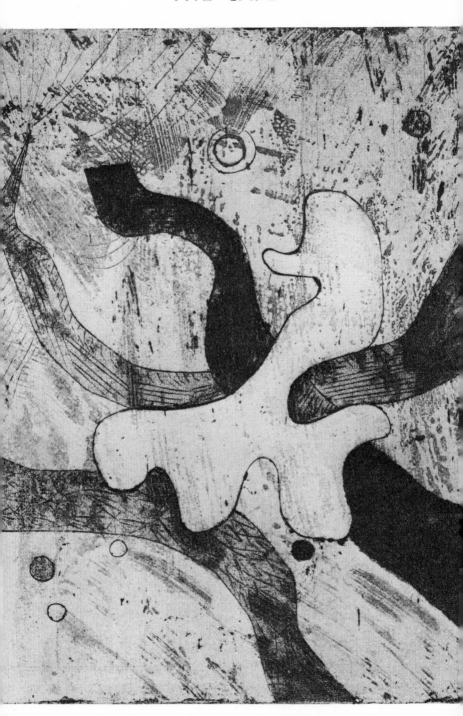

THE CAFÉS were the wells of treasures, the caves of Ali Baba.

The cafés were richer even than the oriental cities where all living was plied openly under your eyes so that you were offered all the activities of the world to touch and smell. You saw your shoes being made from the skinning of the animal to the polishing of the leather. You saw the weaving of cloth and the dyeing in pails of multicolored liquids. You saw the scribes writing letters for the illiterate, the philosopher meditating, the religious man chanting as he squatted and the lepers disintegrating under your eyes, within touch of your hand.

And so in the café, with one franc for a glass of wine and even less for coffee, you could hear stories from the Pampas, share in African voodoo secrets, read the pages of a book being written, listen to a poem, to the death rattles of an aristocrat, the life story of a revolutionary. You could hear the hummed theme of a symphony, watch the fingers of a jazz drummer drumming on the table, accept an invitation from a painter who would take you to the Zoo to watch the serpents eat their daily ration of white mice, consult a secretive Hindu on his explorations of occult streets, or meet an explorer who would take you on his sailboat around the world.

The chill of autumn was tempered by little coal stoves and glass partitions.

A soft rain covered the city with a muted lid, making it intimate like a room, shutting out sky and sun as if drawing curtains, lighting lamps early, kindling fires in the fireplaces, pushing human beings gently to live under the surface, inciting them to sprout words, sparkling colors out of their own flesh, to become light, fire, flowers and tropical fiestas.

The café was the hothouse, densely perfumed with all the banned oils, the censured musks, the richest blooms accelerated by enclosure, warmth, and cross-graftings from all races.

No sunsets, no dawns, but exhibits of paintings rivaling all in luxuriance. Rivers of words, forests of sculptures, huge pyramids of personalities. No need of gardens.

City and cafés became intimate like a room that was carpeted, quilted for the easy intermingling of man's inner landscapes, his multiple secret wishes vibrating from table to table as elbows touched and the *garçon* not only carried brimming glasses but endless messages and signals as the servants did in the old Arabian tales.

Day and night were colliding gently at twilight, throwing off erotic sparks.

Day and night met on the boulevards.

Sabina was always breaking the molds which life formed around her.

She was always trespassing boundaries, erasing identifications.

She could not bear to have a permanent address, to give her telephone number.

Her greatest pleasure consisted in being where no one knew she was, in an out-of-the-way café, a little-known hotel, if possible a room from which the number had been scratched off.

She changed her name as criminals efface their tracks.

She herself did not know what she was preserving from detection, what mystery she was defending.

She hated factual questions as to her activities. Above all she hated to be registered in any of the official books. She hated to give her birth hour, her genealogy, and all her dealings with passport authorities were blurred and complicated.

She lived entirely by a kind of opportunism, all her acts dictated by the demands of the present situation.

She eluded tabulations only to place herself more completely at the disposal of anyone's fantasy about her.

She kept herself free of all identifications the better to obey some stranger's invention about her.

As soon as a man appeared the game began.

She must keep silent. She must let him look at her face and let his dream take form. She must allow time and silence for his invention to develop.

She let him build an image. She saw the image take form in his eyes. If she said what she wanted to say he might think her an ordinary woman!

This image of herself as a *not* ordinary woman, an image which was trembling now in his eyes, might suddenly disappear. Nothing more difficult to live up to than men's dreams. Nothing more tenuous, elusive to fulfill than men's dreams.

She might say the wrong phrase, make the wrong gesture, smile the wrong smile, and then see his eyes waver vulnerably for one instant before turning to the glassy brilliance of disillusion.

She wanted desperately to answer man's most impossible wishes. If the man said: you seem perverse to me, then she would set about gathering together all her knowledge of perversity to become what he had called her.

It made life difficult. She lived the tense, strained life of an international spy. She moved among enemies set on exposing her pretenses. People felt the falseness at times and sought to uncover her.

She had such a fear of being discovered!

She could not bear the light of common, everyday simplicities! As other women blink at the sunlight, she blinked at the light of common everyday simplicities.

And so this race which must never stop. To run from the slanting eyes of one to the caressing hands of another to the sadness of the third.

As she collided with people they lost their identities also: they became objects of desire, objects to be consumed, fuel for the bonfire. Their quality was summarized as either inflammable or noninflammable. That was all that counted. She never distinguished age, nationality, class, fortune, status, occupation or vocation.

Her desire rushed instantaneously, without past or future. A point of fire in the present to which she attached no contracts, no continuity.

Her breasts were always heavy and full. She was like a messenger carrying off all she received from one to carry it to the other, carrying in her breasts the words said to her, the book given her, the land visited, the experience acquired, in the form of stories to be spun continuously.

Everything lived one hour before was a story to tell the following hour to the second companion. From room to room what was perpetuated was her pollen-carrying body.

When someone asked her: where are you going now? whom are you going to meet? she lied. She lied because this current sweeping her onward seemed to cause others pain.

Crossing the street she nourished herself upon the gallant smile of the policeman who stopped the traffic for her. She culled the desire of the man who pushed the revolving door for her. She gathered the flash of adoration from the drugstore clerk: are you an actress? She picked the bouquet of the shoe salesman trying on her shoes: are you a dancer? As she sat in the bus she received the shafts of the sun as a personal intimate visit. She felt a humorous connivance with the truck driver who had to pull the brakes violently before her impulsive passages and who did so smiling.

Every moment this current established itself, this state of flow, of communication by seduction.

She always returned with her arms full of adventures,

as other women return with packages. Her whole body rich with this which nourished her and from which she nourished others. The day finished always too early and she was not empty of restlessness.

Leaning out of the window at dawn, pressing her breasts upon the window sill, she still looked out of the window hoping to see what she had failed to grasp, to possess. She looked at the ending night and the passersby with the keen alertness of the voyager who can never reach terminations as ordinary people reach peaceful terminals at the end of each day, accepting pauses, deserts, rests, havens, as she could not accept them.

She believed only in fire. She wanted to be at every explosion of fire, every convergence of danger. She lived like a fireman, tense for all the emergencies of conflagrations. She was a menace to peaceful homes, tranquil streets.

She was the firebug who was never detected.

Because she believed that fire ladders led to love. This was the motive for her incendiary habits. But Sabina, with all her fire ladders, could not find love.

At dawn she would find herself among ashes again. And so she could not rest or sleep.

As soon as the day dawned peaceful, uneventful,

Sabina slipped into her black satin dress, lacquered her nails the color of her mood, pulled her black cape around her and set out for the cafés.

At dawn Jay turned towards Lillian lying beside him and his first kiss reached her through the net of her hair.

Her eyes were closed, her nerves asleep, but under his hand her body slipped down a dune into warm waves lapping over each other, rippling her skin.

Jay's sensual thrusts wakened the dormant walls of flesh, and tongues of fire flicked towards his hard lashings piercing the kernel of mercury, disrupting a current of fire through the veins. The burning fluid of ecstasy eddying madly and breaking, loosening a river of pulsations.

The core of ecstasy bursting to the rhythmic pounding, until his hard thrusts spurted burning fluid against the walls of flesh, impulsion within the womb like a thunderbolt.

Lillian's panting decreased, and her body reverberated in the silence, filled with echoes . . . antennae which had drunk like the stems of plants.

He awakened free, and she did not.

His desire had reached a finality, like a clean saber cut which dealt pleasure, not death.

She felt impregnated.

She had greater difficulty in shifting, in separating, in turning away.

Her body was filled with retentions, residues, sediments.

He awakened and passed into other realms. The longer his stay in the enfolding whirls, the greater his energy to enter activity again. He awakened and he talked of painting, he awakened laughing, eyes closed with laughter, laughing on the edge of his cheeks, laughter in the corner of his mouth, the laughter of great separateness.

She awakened unfree, as if laden with the seeds of his being, wondering at what moment he would pull his whole self away as one tears a plant out by the roots, leaving a crevice in the earth. Dreading the break because she felt him a master of this act, free to enter and free to emerge, whereas she felt dispossessed of her identity and freedom because Jay upon awakening did not turn about and contemplate her even for a moment as Lillian, a particular woman, but that when he took her, or looked at her he did so gaily, anonymously, as if any woman lying there would have been equally pleasant, natural, and not Lillian among all women.

He was already chuckling at some idea for a painting, already hungry for breakfast, ready to open his mail and embark on multiple relationships, curious about the day's climate, the changes in the street, the detailed news of the brawl of the night before which had taken place under their window.

Fast fast fast moving away, his mind already pursuing the wise sayings of Lao-tse, the theories of Picasso, already like a vast wheel at the fair starting on a wide circle which at no point whatever seemed to include her, because she was there like bread for him, a non-identifiable bread which he ate of as he would eat any bread, not even troubling with the ordinary differentiations: today my bread is fresh and warm, and today it is a little dry, today it lacks salt, today it is lifeless, today it is golden and crisp.

She did not reach out to possess Jay, as he believed, but she reached out because so much of Jay had been deposited, sown, planted within her that she felt possessed, as if she were no longer able to move, breathe, live independently of him. She felt her dependence, lost to herself, given, invaded, and at his mercy, and the anxiety of this, the defenselessness caused a clinging which was the clinging of the drowning. . . .

And if she were bread, she would have liked Jay at least to notice all variations in moods and flavors. She would have liked Jay to say: you are my bread, a very unique and marvelous bread, like none other. If you were not here I would die of instantaneous starvation.

Not at all. If he painted well, it was the spring day. If he were gay it was the Pernod. If he were wise it was the little book of Lao-tse's sayings. If he were elated it was due to a worshipful letter in the mail.

And me, and me, said a small, anxious voice in Lillian's being, where am I?

She was not even the woman in his paintings.

He was painting Sabina. He painted her as a mandrake with fleshly roots, bearing a solitary purple flower in a purple bell-shaped corolla of narcotic flesh. He painted her born with red-gold eyes always burning as from caverns, from holes in the earth, from behind trees. Painted her as one of the luxuriant women, a tropical growth, excommunicated from the bread line as too rich a substance for everyday living, placing her there merely as a denizen of the world of fire, and was content with her intermittent, parabolic appearances.

So, if she were not in his paintings, Lillian thought, where was she? When he finished painting he drank. When he drank he exulted in his powers and palmed it all on the holy ghost inside of him, each time calling the spirit animating him by a different name that was not Lillian. Today it was the holy ghost, and the spring light and a dash of Pernod.

He did not say what Lillian wanted to hear: "You are the holy ghost inside of me. You make my spring."

She was not even sure of that—of being his holy ghost. At times it seemed to her that he was painting with Djuna's eyes. When Djuna was there he painted better. He did not paint her. He only felt strong and capable when he tackled huge masses, strong features, heavy bodies. Djuna's image was too tenuous for him.

But when she was there he painted better.

Silently she seemed to be participating, silently she seemed to be transmitting forces.

Where did her force come from? No one knew.

She merely sat there and the colors began to organize themselves, to deepen, as if he took the violet from her eyes when she was angry, the blue when she was at peace, the gray when she was detached, the gold when she was melted and warm, and painted with them. Using her eyes as a color chart.

In this way he passed from the eyes of Lillian which said: "I am here to warm you." Eyes of devotion.

To the eyes of Sabina which said: "I am here to consume you."

To the eyes of Djuna which said: "I am here to reflect your painter's dream, like a crystal ball."

Bread and fire and light, he needed them all. He could be nourished on Lillian's faith but it did not illumine his work. There were places into which Lillian could not follow him. When he was tormented by a half-formed image he went to Djuna, just as once walking through the streets with her he had seen a child bring her a tangled skein of string to unravel.

He would have liked the three women to love each other. It seemed to him that then he would be at peace. When they pulled against each other for supremacy it was as if different parts of his own body pulled against each other.

On days when Lillian accepted understanding through the eyes of Djuna, when each one was connected with her role and did not seek to usurp the other's place he was at peace and slept profoundly.

(If only, thought Lillian, lying in the disordered bed, when he moved away I could be quiet and complete and free. He seems bound to me and then so completely unbound. He changes. One day I look at him and there is warmth in him, and the next a kind of ruthlessness. There are times when he kisses me and I feel he is not kissing me but any woman, or all the women he has known. There are times when he seems made of wax, and I can see on him the imprint of all those he has seen during the day. I can hear their words. Last night he even fraternized with the man who was courting me. What does this mean? Even with Edgar who was trying to take me away from him. He was in one of his moods of effusive display, when he loved everybody. He is promiscuous. I can't bear how near they come, they talk in his face, they breathe his breath. Anyone at all has this privilege. Anyone can talk to him, share his house, and even me. He gives away everything. Djuna says I lack faith. . . . Is that what it is? But how can I heal myself? I thought one could get healed by just living and loving.)

Lying in bed and listening to Jay whistling while he shaved in the bathroom, Lillian wondered why she felt simultaneously in bondage and yet unmarried, unappeased, and all her conversations with Djuna with whom she was able to talk even better than to monologize with herself once more recurred to her before she allowed herself to face the dominant impulse ruling her: to run away from Jay.

Passion gathered its momentum, its frenzy, from the effort to possess what was unpossessable in reality, because it sprang from an illusion, because it gained impetus from a secret knowledge of its unfulfillable quality, because it attacked romantic organisms, and incited to fever in place of a natural union by feelings. Passion between two people came from a feverish desire to fuse elements which were unfusable. The extreme heat to which human beings subjected themselves in this experiment, as if by intensity the unfusable elements could be melted into one—water with fire, fire with earth, rock and water. An effort doomed to defeat.

Lillian could not see all this, but felt it happening, and knew that this was why she had wept so bitterly at their first quarrel: not weeping over a trivial difference but because her instinct warned her senses that this small difference indicated a wider one, a difference of elements, by which the relationship would ultimately be destroyed.

In one of his cheerful, human moods Jay had said: "If my friends bother you so much, we shall put them all against a wall and shoot them."

But Lillian knew that if today Jay surrendered today's set of friends, he would renew the same kind of relationships with a new set, for they reflected the part of him she did not feel close to, the part in fact she was at war with.

Lillian's disproportionate weeping had seemed childish

to Jay who saw only the immediate difference, but Lillian was weeping blindly with a fear of death of the relationship, with her loss of faith sensing the first fissure as the first symbol of future dissolution, and knowing from that moment on that the passion between them would no longer be an affirmation of marriage but a struggle against death and separation.

(Djuna said: You can't bear to let this relationship die. But why must it die, Djuna? Do you believe all passion must die? Is there nothing I can do to avoid failure? Passion doesn't die of natural death. Everyone says passion dies, love dies, but it's we who kill it. Djuna believes this, Djuna said: You can fight all the symptoms of divorce when they first appear, you can be on your guard against distortions, against the way people wound each other and instill doubt, you can fight for the life and continuity of this passion, there *is* a knowledge which postpones the death of a relationship, death is not natural, but, Lillian, you cannot do it alone, there are seeds of death in his character, one cannot fight alone for a living relationship. It takes the effort of two. Effort, effort. The word most foreign to Jay. Jay would never make an effort. Djuna, Djuna, couldn't you talk to him? Djuna, will you talk to him? No, it's useless, he does not want anything that is difficult to reach. He does not like effort or struggles. He wants only his pleasure. It isn't possessiveness, Djuna, but I want to feel at the center so that I can allow him the maximum freedom without feeling each time that he betrays everything, destroys everything.)

She would run away.

When Jay saw her dressing, powdering her face, pulling up her stockings, combing her hair, he noticed no change in her gestures to alarm him, for did she not always comb her hair and powder and dress with the flurry of a runaway. Wasn't she always so uneasy and overquick, as if she had been frightened?

He went to his studio and Lillian locked the door of the bedroom and sat at her piano, to seek in music that wholeness which she could not find in love. . . .

Just as the sea often carries bodies, wrecks, shells, lost objects carved by the sea itself in its own private studio of sculpture to unexpected places, led by irrational currents, just so did the current of music eject fragments of the self believed drowned and deposited them on the shore altered, recarved, rendered anonymous in shape. Each backwash, each crosscurrent, throwing up new material formed out of the old, from the ocean of memories.

Driftwood figures that had been patiently recarved by

the sea with rhythms broken by anger, patiently remolding forms to the contours of knotted nightmares, woods stunted and distorted by torments of doubts.

She played until this flood of debris rose from the music to choke her, closed the piano with anger, and rose to plan her escape.

Escape. Escape.

Her first instinctive, blind gesture of escape was to don the black cape copied from Sabina's at the time of their relationship.

She wrapped Sabina's cape around her, and put two heavy bracelets around her wrist (one for each wrist, not wanting any more to be in bondage to one, never to one; she would split the desire in two, to rescue one half of herself from destruction).

And for the first time since her marriage to Jay, she climbed the worn stairs of a very old hotel in Montparnasse, experiencing the exaltation familiar to runaways.

The more she could see of the worn carpet and its bare skeleton, the more acrid the smell of poverty, the more bare the room, this which might have lowered the diapason of another's mood only increased the elation of hers, becoming transfigured by her conviction that she was making a voyage which would forever take her away from the prison of anxiety, the pain of dependence on a human being she could not trust. Her mood of liberation spangled and dappled shabbiness with light like an impressionist painting.

Her sense of familiarity with this scene did not touch her at first: a lover was waiting for her in one of the rooms of this hotel.

Could anyone help her to forget Jay for a moment? Could Edgar help her, Edgar with his astonished eyes saying to her: You are wonderful, you are wonderful! Drunkenly repeating you are wonderful! as they danced under Jay's very eyes not seeing, not seeing her dancing with Edgar in the luminous spotlight of a night club, but when her dress opened a little at the throat she could smell the mixed odor of herself and Jay.

She was taking revenge now for his effusive confessions as to the pleasures he had taken with other women.

She had been made woman by Jay, he alone held in his hands all the roots of her being, and when he had pulled them, in his own limitless motions outward and far, he had inflicted such torture that he had destroyed the roots all at once and sent her into space, sent her listening to Edgar's words gratefully, grateful for Edgar's hands on her pulling her away from Jay, grateful for his foolish gift of flowers in silver paper (because Jay gave her no gifts at all), and she would imagine Jay watching this scene, watching her go up the stairs to Edgar's room, wearing flowers in a silver paper, and she enjoyed imagining his pain, as he witnessed the shedding of her clothes, witnessed her lying down beside Edgar. (You are the man of the crowd, Jay, and so I lie here beside a stranger. What makes me lonely, Jay, are the cheap and gaudy people you are friendly with, and I lie here with a stranger who is only caressing you inside of me. He is complaining like a woman: you are not thinking of me, you are not filled with me.)

But no sooner had she shed her cape copied from Sabina's than she recognized the room, the man, the scene, and the feelings as not belonging to her, not having been selected by her, but as having been borrowed from Sabina's repertoire of stories of adventures.

Lillian was not free of Jay since she had invited him to witness the scene enacted solely to punish his unfaithfulness. She was not free, she was being Sabina, with the kind of man Sabina would have chosen. All the words and gestures prescribed by Sabina in her feverish descriptions, for thus was much experience transmitted by contagion, and Lillian, not yet free, had been more than others predisposed to the contagion by lowered resistance!

She was ashamed, not of the sensual meeting, but for having acted in disguise, and eluded responsibility.

When the stranger asked her for her name she did not say Lillian, but Sabina.

She returned home to shed her cape and her acts, pretending not to know this woman who had spent hours with a stranger.

To put the responsibility on Sabina.

Escape escape escape—into what? Into borrowing the self of Sabina for an hour. She had donned the recklessness of Sabina, borrowed her cape for a shy masquerade, pretending freedom.

The clothes had not fitted very well.

But after a while, would this cease to be a role and did the borrowing reveal Lillian's true desires?

The possibility of being this that she borrowed.

Blindly ashamed of what she termed unfaithfulness (when actually she was still so tied to Jay it was merely within the precincts of their relationship that she could act, with his presence, and therefore unsevered from him), she discarded all the elements of this charade, cape, bracelets, then bathed and dressed in her own Lillian costume and went to the café where she sat beside Sabina who had already accumulated several plates by which the waiter was able to add the number of drinks.

When Jay felt exhausted after hours of painting he went to see Djuna.

He always softened as he thought of Djuna. She was to him more than a woman. It had been difficult at first to see her simply as a woman. His first impression had been an association with Florentine painting, his feeling that no matter what her origin, her experiences, her resemblances to other women, she was for him like a canvas which had been covered first of all with a coating of gold paint, so that whatever one painted over it, this gold on which he had dissertated during one of his early visits to her, was present as it remained present in the Florentine paintings.

But even though his obsession for dispelling illusions, which made him pull at her eyelashes to see if they were real, which made him open jars and bottles in the bathroom to see what they contained, even though he always had the feeling that women resorted to tricks and contrived spells which man must watch out for, he still felt that she was more than a woman, and that given the

134

right moment, she was willing to shed the veils, the elusiveness, and to be completely honest.

It was not her clarity either, which he called honesty. Her clarity he distrusted. She always made wonderful patterns—he admitted that. There was a kind of Grecian symmetry to her movements, her life, and her words. They looked convincingly harmonious, clear—too clear. And in the meanwhile where was she? Not on the clear orderly surface of her ideas any longer, but submerged, sunk in some obscure realm like a submarine. She had only appeared to give you all her thoughts. She had only seemed to empty herself in this clarity. She gave you a neat pattern and then slipped out of it herself and laughed at you. Or else she gave you a neat pattern and then slipped out of it herself and then the utterly tragic expression of her face testified to some other realm she had entered and not allowed one to follow her into, a realm of despair even, a realm of anguish, which was only betrayed by her eyes.

What was the mystery of woman? Only this obstinacy in concealing themselves—merely this persistence in creating mysteries, as if the exposure of her thoughts and feelings were gifts reserved for love and intimacy.

He suspected that some day an honest woman would

clear all this away. He never suspected for a moment that this mystery was a part of themselves they did not know, could not see.

Djuna, he ruminated, was a more ornamented woman, but an honest one.

He had long ago found a way to neutralize the potencies of woman by a simplification all his own, which was to consider all women as sharing but one kind of hunger, a hunger situated between the two pale columns of the legs. Even the angels, said Jay, even the angels, and the mothers, and the sisters, were all made the same way, and he retained this focus upon them from the time when he was a very little boy playing on the floor of his mother's kitchen and an enormous German woman had come straight to them from the immigration landing, still wearing her voluminous peasant skirts, her native costume, and she had stood in the kitchen asking his mother to help her find work, using some broken jargon impossible to understand—everyone in the house dismayed by her foreignness, her braids, her speech. As if to prove her capabilities through some universal gesture, she had started to knead the dough expertly, kneading with fervor, while Jay's mother watched her with increasing interest.

Jay was playing on the floor with matches, unnoticed,

and he found himself covered as by a huge and colorful tent by the perfoliate skirt of the German woman, his glance lost where two pale columns converged in a revelation which had given him forever this perspective of woman's being, this vantage point of insight, this observatory and infallible focus, which prevented him from losing his orientation in the vastest maze of costumes, classes, races, nationalities—no external variations able to deprive him of this intimate knowledge of woman's most secret architecture. . . .

Chuckling, he thought of Djuna's expression whenever she opened the door to receive him.

The dreamer wears fur and velvet blinkers.

Chuckling, Jay thought of himself entering the house, and of her face shining between these blinkers of her vision of him as a great painter, shutting out with royal indifference all other elements which might disturb this vision.

He could see on her face this little shrine built by the dreamer in which she placed him as a great painter. Won by her fervor, he would enter with her into her dream of him, and begin to listen raptly to her way of transmuting into gold everything he told her!

If he had stolen from the Zombie's pocketbook she said it was because the Zombie was provocatively

137

miserly. If he complained that he was oversleeping when he should be working Djuna translated it that he was catching up on sleep lost during the period when he had only a moving-picture hall to sleep in.

She only heard and saw what she wanted to hear and see. (Damn women!) Her expression of expectancy, of faith, her perpetual absolution of his acts disconcerted him at times.

The more intently he believed all she believed while he was with her, the more precipitately he fell out of grace when he left her, because he felt she was the depository of his own dream, and that she would keep it while he turned his back on it.

One of the few women, chuckled Jay, who understood the artificial paradise of art, the language of man.

As he walked the city took on the languid beauty of a woman, which was the beauty of Paris, especially at five o'clock, at twilight, when the fountains, the parks, the soft lighting, the humid streets like blue mirrors, all dissolved into a haze of pearl, extending their fripperies and coquetries.

At the same hour New York took on its masculine and aggressive beauty, with its brash lighting, its steel arrows and giant obelisks piercing the sky, an electric erectness, a rigid city pitiless to lovers, sending detectives to hotel rooms to track them down, at the same hour that the French waiter said to the couples: do you wish a *cabinet particular*—at the same hour that in New York all the energies were poured into steel structures, digging oil wells, harnessing electricity, for power.

Jay walked leisurely, like a ragpicker of good moments, walked through streets of joy, throwing off whatever disturbed him, gathering only what pleased him, noticing with delight that the washed and faded blue of the café awning matched the washed faded blue face of the clock in the church spire.

Then he saw the café table where Lillian sat talking with Sabina, and knowing his dream of becoming a great painter securely stored in the eyes of Djuna (damn women!) he decided to sin against it by sinking into the more shallow fantasies born of absinthe.

Djuna awakened from so deep a dream that opening her eyes was like pushing aside a heavy shroud of veils, a thousand layers of veils, and with a sensation similar to that of the trapezist who has been swinging in vast spaces, and suddenly feels again in his two hands the coarse touch of the swing cord.

She awakened fully to the painful knowledge that this was a day when she would be possessed by a mood which cut her off from fraternity.

It was also at those moments that she would have the clearest intuitions, sudden contacts with the deepest selves of others, divine the most hidden sorrow.

But if she spoke from this source, others would feel uneasy, not recognizing the truth of what she said. They always felt exposed and were quick to revenge themselves. They rushed to defend this exposure of the self they did not know, they were not familiar with, or did not like. They blamed her for excess of imagination, for exaggeration.

They persisted in living on familiar terms only with the surface of their personalities, and what she reached lay deeper where they could not see it. They felt at ease among their falsities, and the nakedness of her insight seemed like forcing open underworlds whose entrance was tacitly barred in everyday intercourse.

They would accuse her of living in a world of illusion while they lived in reality.

Their falsities had such an air of solidity, entirely supported by the palpable.

But she felt that on the contrary, she had contact with

their secret desires, secret fears, secret intents. And she had faith in what she saw.

She attributed all her difficulties merely to the over-quickness of her rhythm. Proofs would always follow later, too late to be of value to her human life, but not too late to be added to this city of the interior she was constructing, to which none had access.

Yet she was never surprised when people betrayed the self she saw, which was this maximum rendition of themselves. This maximum she knew to be a torment, this knowledge of all one might achieve, become, was a threat to human joy and life. She felt in sympathy with those who turned their back on it. Yet she also knew that if they did, another torment awaited them: that of having fallen short of their own dream.

She would have liked to escape from her own demands upon herself.

But even if at times she was taken with a desire to become blind, to drift, to abandon her dreams, to slip into negation, destruction, she carried in herself something which altered the atmosphere she sought and which proved stronger than the place or people she had permitted to infect her with their disintegration, their betrayal of their original dream of themselves.

Even when she let herself be poisoned with all that was human, defeat, jealousy, sickness, surrender, blindness, she carried an essence which was like a counterpoison and which reversed despair into hope, bitterness into faith, abortions into births, weight into lightness.

Everything in her hands changed substance, quality, form, intent.

Djuna could see it happen against her will, and did not know why it happened.

Was it because she began every day anew as children do, without memory of defeat, rancor, without memory of disaster? No matter what happened the day before, she always awakened with an expectation of a miracle. Her hands always appeared first from out of the sheets, hands without memories, wounds, weights, and these hands danced.

That was her awakening. A new day was a new life. Every morning was a beginning.

No sediments of pain, sadness yes, but no stagnating pools of accumulated bitterness.

Djuna believed one could begin anew as often as one dared.

The only acid she contained was one which dissolved the calluses formed by life around the sensibilities.

Every day she looked at people with the eyes of faith.

Placing an unlimited supply of faith at their disposal. Since she did not accept the actual self as final, seeing only the possibilities of expansion, she established a climate of infinite possibilities.

She did not mind that by this expectation of a miracle, she exposed herself to immense disappointments. What she suffered as a human being when others betrayed themselves and her she counted as nothing—like the pains of childbirth.

She believed that the dream which human beings carry in themselves was man's greatest hunger. If statistics were taken there would be found more deaths by aborted dreams than from physical calamities, more deaths by dream abortions than child abortions, more deaths by infection from despair than from physical illness.

Carrying this ultimate knowledge she was often the victim of strange revenges: people's revenge against the image of their unfulfilled dream. If they could annihilate her they might annihilate this haunting image of their completed selves and be done with it!

She only knew one person who might rescue her from this world, from this city of the interior lying below the level of identity.

She might learn from Jay to walk into a well-peopled world and abandon the intense selectivity of the dream (*this* personage fits into my dream and this one does not).

The dreamer rejects the ordinary.

Jay invited the ordinary. He was content with unformed fragments of people, incomplete ones: a minor doctor, a feeble painter, a mediocre writer, an average of any kind.

For Djuna it must always be: an extraordinary doctor, a unique writer, a summation of some kind, which could become a symbol by its completeness, by its greatness in its own realm.

Jay was the living proof that it was in this acceptance of the ordinary that pleasure lay. She would learn from him. She would learn to like daily bread. He gave her everything in its untransformed state: food, houses, streets, cafés, people. A way back to the simplicities.

Somewhere, in the labyrinth of her life, bread had been transformed on her tongue into a wafer, with the imponderability of symbols. Communion had been the actual way she experienced life—as communion, not as bread and wine. In place of bread the wafer, in place of blood, the wine.

Jay would give her back a crowded world untransmuted. He had mocked her once saying he had found her portrait in one page of the dictionary under *Trans:* transmutations, transformation, transmitting etc.

In the world of the dreamer there was solitude: all the exaltations and joys came in the moment of preparation for living. They took place in solitude. But with action came anxiety, and the sense of insuperable effort made to match the dream, and with it came weariness, discouragement, and the flight into solitude again. And then in solitude, in the opium den of remembrance, the possibility of pleasure again.

What was she seeking to salvage from the daily current of living, what sudden revulsions drove her back into the solitary cell of the dream?

Let Jay lead her out of the cities of the interior.

She would work as usual, hours of dancing, then she would take her shoes to be repaired, then she would go to the café.

The shoemaker was working with his window open on the street. As often as Djuna passed there he would be sitting in his low chair, his head bowed over his work, a nail between his lips, a hammer in his hand.

She took all her shoes to him for repairing, because he had as great a love of unique shoes as she did. She brought him slippers from Montenegro whose tips were raised like the prows of galleys, slippers from Morocco embroidered in gold thread, sandals from Thibet.

His eyes traveled up from his work towards the

package she carried as if she were bringing him a gift.

He took the fur boots from Lapland he had not seen before, and was moved by the simplicity of their sewing, the reindeer guts sewn by hand. He asked for their history.

Djuna did not have to explain to him that as she could not travel enough to satisfy the restlessness of her feet, she could at least wear shoes which came from the place she might never visit. She did not have to explain to him that when she looked at her feet in Lapland boots she felt herself walking through deserts of snow.

The shoes carried her everywhere, tireless shoes walking forever all over the world.

This shoemaker repaired them with all the curiosity of a great traveler. He respected the signs of wear and tear as if she were returning from all the voyages she had wanted to make. It was not alone the dust or mud of Paris he brushed off but of Egypt, Greece, India. Every shoe she brought him was his voyage too. He respected wear as a sign of distance, broken straps as an indication of discoveries, torn heels as an accident happening only to explorers.

He was always sitting down. From his cellar room he looked up at the window where he could see only the feet of the passers-by.

"I love a foot that has elegance," he said. "Sometimes for days I see only ugly feet. And then perhaps one pair of beautiful feet. And that makes me happy."

As Djuna was leaving, for the first time he left his low working chair and moved forward to open the door for her, limping.

He had a club foot.

Once she had been found in the corner of a room by her very angry parents, all covered by a shawl. Their anxiety in not finding her for a long time, turned to great anger.

"What are you doing there hiding, covered by a shawl?"

She answered: "Traveling. I am traveling."

The Rue de la Sante, the Rue Dolent, the Rue des Saint Peres became Bombay, Ladoma, Budapest, Lavinia.

The cities of the interior were like the city of Fez, intricate, endless, secret and unchartable.

Then she saw Jay sitting at the café table with Lillian, Donald, Michael, Sabina and Rango, and she joined them.

Faustin the Zombie, as everyone called him, awakened in a room he thought he had selected blindly but which gave the outward image of his inner self as accurately as if he had turned every element of himself into a carpet or a piece of furniture.

First of all it was not accessible to the door when it opened, but had to be reached by a dark and twisted corridor. Then he had contrived to cover the windows in such a manner with a glazed material that the objects, books and furniture appeared to be conserved in a storage room, to be at once dormant and veiled. The odor they emitted was the odor of hibernation.

One expected vast hoods to fall over the chairs and couch. Certain chairs were dismally isolated and had to be forcibly dragged to enter into relation with other chairs. There was an inertia in the pillows, an indifference in the wilted texture of the couch cover. The table in the center of the room blocked all passageways, the lamp shed a tired light. The walls absorbed the light without throwing it back.

His detachment affected the whole room. Objects need human warmth like human beings to bloom. A lamp sheds a meager or a prodigal light according to one's interior lighting. Even specks of dust are inhabited by the spirit of the master. There are rooms in which even the dust is brilliant. There are rooms in which even carelessness is alive, as the disorder of someone rushing to more important matters. But here in Faustin's room, there was not even the disorder caused by emotional draughts!

The walls of the rooming house were very thin, and he could hear all that took place in the other rooms.

This morning he awakened to a clear duet between a man and a woman.

Man: It's unbelievable, we've been together six years now, and I still have an illusion about you! I've never had this as long with any woman.

Woman: Six years!

Man: I'd like to know how often you have been unfaithful.

Woman: Well, I don't want to know how many times you were.

Man: Oh, me, only a few times. Whenever you went away and I'd get lonely and angry that you had left me. One summer at the beach . . . do you remember the model Colette?

Woman: I didn't ask you. I don't want to know.

Man: But I do. I know you went off with that singer. Why did you? A singer. I couldn't make love to a singer!

Woman: But you made love to a model.

Man: That's different. You know it's not important. You know you're the only one.

Woman: You'd think it was important if I had.

Man: It's different for a woman. Why? Why did you, what made you go with that singer, why, when I love you so much and desire you so often?

Silence.

Woman: I don't believe we should talk about this. I don't want to know about you. (Crying) I never wanted to think about it, and now you made me.

Man: You're crying! But it's nothing. I forgot it immediately. And in six years only a few times. Whereas you, I'm sure it was many times.

Woman: (still crying) I didn't ask you. Why did you have to tell me?

Man: I'm just more sincere than you are.

149

Woman: It isn't sincerity, it's revenge. You told me just to hurt me.

Man: I told you because I thought it would drive you into being honest with me.

Silence.

Man: How obstinate you are. Why are you crying?

Woman: Not over your unfaithfulness!

Man: Over your own then?

Woman: I'm crying over unfaithfulness in general—how people hurt each other.

Man: Unfaithfulness in general! What a fine way to evade the particular.

Silence.

Man: I'd like to know how you learned all you know about love-making. Who did you learn from? You know what very few women do.

Woman: I learned . . . from talking with other women. I also have a natural gift.

Man: I suppose it was Maurice who taught you the most. It enrages me to see how much you know.

Woman: I never asked you where you learned. Besides, it's always personal. Each couple invents their own way.

Man: Yes, that's true. Sometimes I made you cry with joy, didn't I?

Woman: (crying) Why do you use the past tense?

Man: Why did you go off with that singer?

Woman: If you insist so much I will tell you something.

Man: (in a very tense voice) About the singer?

Woman: No, someone else. Once I tried to be unfaithful. You were neglecting me. I took rather a fancy to someone. And all might have gone well except that he had the same habit you have of starting with: you have the softest skin in the world. And when he said this, just as you do, I remembered your saying that, and I left the man, I ran away. Nothing happened.

Man: But just the same he had time to note the quality of your skin.

Woman: I'm telling you the truth.

Man: You have nothing to cry about now. You have taken your revenge.
Woman: I'm crying about unfaithfulness in general, all the betrayals.
Man: I will never forgive you.
Woman: Once in six years!
Man: I'm sure it was that singer.

Faustin, lying down, smoking as he listened, felt the urgent need to comment. He knocked angrily on the wall. The man and the woman were silent.

"Listen," he said, in his loudest voice," I heard your entire conversation. I would say in this case the man is very unjust and the woman right. She was more faithful than the man. She was faithful to a personal emotion, to a personal rite."

"Who are you?" said the man in the other room, angrily.

"No one in particular, just a neighbor.'"

There was a long silence. Then the sound of a door being closed violently. Faustin heard one person moving about with soft rustles. Judging from the steps, it was the man who had gone out.

Faustin lay down again, meditating on his own anxiety.

He felt at this moment like a puppet, but he became aware that all this had happened many times before to him, but never as clearly.

All living had taken place for him in the other room,

and he had always been the witness. He had always been the commentator.

He felt a guilt for having listened, which was like the guilt he felt at other times for never being the one in action. He was always accompanying someone to a marriage, not his own, to a hospital, to a burial, to a celebration in which he played no part but that of the accompanist.

He was allowing them all to live for him, and then articulating a judgment. He was allowing Jay to paint for him, and then he was the one to write ironic articles on his exhibits. He was allowing Sabina to devastate others with her passion, and smiling at those who were consumed or rejected. Now at this moment he was ashamed not to be the one consumed or rejected. He allowed Djuna to speak, Michael to face the tragic consequences of his deviations in love. He was allowing others to cry, to complain, to die.

And all he did was to speak across a protective wall, to knock with anger and say: you are right, and you are wrong.

Rendered uneasy by these meditations, he dressed himself and decided to go to the café.

———

He was called Uncle Philip by everyone, even by those who were not related to him.

He had the solicitous walk of an undertaker, the unctuous voice of a floorwalker.

His hands were always gloved, his heels properly resoled, his umbrella sheathed.

It was impossible to imagine him having been a child, or even an adolescent. It was admitted he possessed no photographs of that period, and that he had the taste never to talk about this obviously nonexistent facet of his personality. He had been born gray-haired, slender and genteel.

Attired in the most neutral suit, with the manners of someone about to announce a bereavement, Uncle Philip nevertheless did not fulfill such threats and was merely content to register and report minutely on the activity of the large, colorful, international family to which he was related.

No one could mention a country where Uncle Philip did not have a relative who . . .

No one could mention any world, social, political, artistic, financial, political, in which Uncle Philip did not possess a relative who . . .

No one ever thought of inquiring into his own vocation. One accepted him as a witness.

153

By an act of polite prestidigitation and punctuality, Uncle Philip managed to attend a ceremony in India where one of the members of the family was decorated for high bravery. He could give all the details of the function with a precision of colors resembling scenes from the *National Geographic Magazine*.

And a few days later he was equally present at the wedding of another member in Belgium, from which he brought back observations on the tenacious smell of Catholic incense.

A few days later he was present as godfather of a newborn child in Hungary and then proceeded to attend in Paris the first concert of importance given by still another relative.

Amiable and courteous as he shared in the backstage celebrations, he remained immune to the contagion of colors, gaiety and fame. His grayness took no glow from the success, flowers, and handshakes. His pride in the event was historical, and shed no light on his private life.

He was the witness.

He felt neither honored nor disgraced (he also attended death by electric chair of a lesser member).

He appeared almost out of incognito, as a family spirit must, and immediately after the ceremony, after he partook of the wine, food, rice, sermon or verdict, he vanished as he had come and no one remembered him.

He who had traveled a thousand miles to sustain this family tree, to solder the spreading and dissipated family unity, was instantly forgotten.

Of course it was simple enough to follow the careers of the more official members of the family, those who practiced orthodox marriages and divorces, or such classical habits as first nights, presentations at the Court of England, decorations from the Academie Francaise. All this was announced in the papers and all Uncle Philip had to do was to read the columns carefully every morning.

But his devotion to the family did not limit itself to obvious attendance upon the obvious incidents of the family tree. He was not content with appearing at cemeteries, churches, private homes, sanatoriums, hospitals.

He pursued with equal flair and accuracy the more mysterious developments. When one relative entered upon an irregular union Uncle Philip was the first to call, assuming that all was perfectly in order and insisting on all the amenities.

The true mystery lay in the contradiction that the brilliance of these happenings (for even the performance at the electric chair was not without its uniqueness, the electric power failing to achieve its duty) never imparted any radiation to Uncle Philip; that while he moved in a profusion of family-tree blossoms, yet each year he became a little more faded, a little more automatic, a little more starched—like a wooden figure representing irreparable ennui.

His face remained unvaryingly gray, his suits frayed evenly, his soles thinned smoothly, his gloves wore out not finger by finger but all at once, as they should.

He remained alert to his duties, however. His genius for detecting step by step the most wayward activities led him to his most brilliant feat of all.

One relative having wanted to travel across the Atlantic with a companion who was not her husband, deceived all her friends as to the date of her sailing and boarded a ship leaving a day earlier.

As she walked up and down the deck with her compromising escort, thinking regretfully of the flowers, fruit and books which would be delivered elsewhere and lost to her, she encountered Uncle Philip holding a small bouquet and saying in an appropriate voice: "*Bon voyage!* Give my regards to the family when you get to America!"

The only surprising fact was that Uncle Philip failed to greet them at their arrival on the other side.

"Am I aging?" asked Uncle Philip of himself as he awakened, picked up the newspaper at his door, the breakfast tray, and went back to his bed.

He was losing his interest in genealogical trees.

He thought of the café and of all the people he had seen there, watched, listened to. From their talk they seemed to have been born without parents, without relatives. They had all run away, forgotten, or separated from the past. None of them acknowledged parents, or even nationalities.

When he questioned them they were irritated with him, or fled from him.

He thought they were rootless, and yet he felt they were bound to each other, and related to each other as if they had founded new ties, a new kind of family, a new country.

He was the lonely one, he the *esprit de famille*.

The sap that ran through the family tree had not bloomed in him as the sap that ran through these people as they sat together.

He wanted to get up and dress and sit with them. He remembered a painting he had seen in a book of mythology. All in coral and gold, a vast tree, and sitting at each tip of a branch, a mythological personage, man, woman, child, priest or poet, scribe, lyre player, dancer, goddess, god, all sitting in the same tree with a mysterious complacency of unity.

When Donald had been ejected from his apartment because he had not been able to pay his rent, all of them had come in the night and formed a chain and helped him to move his belongings out of the window, and the only danger had been one of discovery due to their irrepressible laughter.

When Jay sold a painting he came to the café to celebrate and that night everyone ate abundantly.

When Lillian gave a concert they all went together forming a compact block of sympathy with effusive applause.

When Stella was invited by some titled person or other to stay at a mansion in the south of France, she invited them all.

When the ballet master fell ill with asthma and could no longer teach dancing, he was fed by all of them.

There was another kind of family, and Uncle Philip wished he could discover the secret of their genealogy.

With this curosity he dressed and went off to the café.

Michael liked to awaken first and look upon the face of Donald asleep on the pillows, as if he could extract from the reality of Donald's face asleep on pillow within reach of his hand, a certitude which might quieten his anxiety, a certitude which once awake Donald would proceed to destroy gradually all through the day and evening.

At no time when he was awake could Donald dispense the word Michael needed, dispense the glance, the smallest act to prove his love.

Michael's feelings at that moment exactly resembled Lillian's feelings in regard to Jay.

Like Lillian he longed for some trivial gift that would prove Donald had wanted to make him a gift. Like Lillian he longed for a word he could enclose within his being that would place him at the center. Like Lillian he longed for some moment of passionate intensity that would be like those vast fires in the iron factory from which the iron emerged incandescent, welded, complete.

He had to be content with Donald asleep upon his pillow.

With Donald's presence.

But no sooner would his eyes open than Donald would proceed to weave a world as inaccessible to Michael as the protean, fluid world of Jay become inaccessible to Lillian.

This weaving began always with Donald's little songs

of nonsense with which he established the mood of the day on a pitch too light for Michael to seize, and which he sang not to please himself, but with a note of defiance, of provocation to Michael:

> Nothing is lost but it changes
> into the new string old string
> into the new bag old bag . . .

"Michael," said Donald, "today I would like to go to the Zoo and see the new weasel who cried so desperately when she was left alone."

Michael thought: "How human of him to feel sympathy for the weasel crying in solitude in its cage." And Donald's sympathy for the weasel encouraged him to say tenderly: "Would you cry like that if you were left alone?"

"Not at all," said Donald, "I wouldn't mind at all. I like to be alone."

"You wouldn't mind if I left you?"

Donald shrugged his shoulders and sang:

> in the new pan old tin
> in the new shoe old leather
> in the new silk old hair
> in the new hat old straw . . .

"Anyhow," said Donald, "what I like best in the Zoo is not the weasel, it's the rhinoceros with his wonderful tough hide."

160

Michael felt inexplicably angry that Donald should like the rhinoceros and not the weasel. That he should admire the toughness of the rhinoceros skin, as if he were betraying him, expressing the wish that Michael should be less vulnerable.

How how how could Michael achieve invulnerability when every gesture Donald made was in a different rhythm from his own, when he remained uncapturable even at the moments when he gave himself.

Donald was singing:

> in the new man the child
> and the new not new
> the new not new
> the new not new

Then he sat down to write a letter and the way he wrote his letter was so much in the manner of a school-boy, with the attentiveness born of awkwardness, an unfamiliarity with concentration, an impatience to have the task over and done with that the little phrase in his song which Michael had not allowed to become audible to his heart now became louder and more ominous: in the new man the child.

As Donald sat biting the tip of his pen, Michael could see him preparing to trip, skip, prance, laugh, but always within a circle in which he admitted no partner.

To avoid the assertion of a difference which would be emphasized in a visit to the Zoo, Michael tempted Donald with a visit to the Flea Market, knowing this to be one of Donald's favorite rambles.

There, exposed in the street, on the sidewalk, lay all the objects the imagination could produce and summon.

All the objects of the world with the added patina of having been possessed already, loved and hated, worn and discarded.

But there, as Michael moved and searched deliberately he discovered a rare book on astronomy, and Donald found the mechanism of a music box without the box, just a skeleton of fine wires that played delicately in the palm of his hand. Donald placed it to his ear to listen and then said: "Michael, buy me this music box. I love it."

In the open air it was scarcely audible, but Donald did not offer it to Michael's ear, as if he were listening to a music not made for him.

Michael bought it for him as one buys a toy for a child, a toy one is not expected to share. And for himself he bought the book on astronomy which Donald did not even glance at.

Donald walked with the music box playing inside of his pocket, and then he wanted reindeer horns, and he wanted a Louis Fifteenth costume, and he wanted an opium pipe.

Michael studied old prints, and all his gestures were slow and lagging with a kind of sadness which Donald refused to see, which was meant to say: "Take me by the hand and let me share your games."

Could he not see, in Michael's bearing, a child imprisoned wishing to keep pace with Donald, wishing to keep pace with his prancing, wishing to hear the music of the music box?

Finally they came upon the balloon woman, holding a floating bouquet of emerald-green balloons, and Donald wanted them all.

"All?" said Michael in dismay.

"Maybe they will carry me up in the air. I'm so much lighter than the old woman," said Donald.

But when he had taken the entire bunch from the woman, and held them and was not lifted off the ground as he expected, he let them fly off and watched their ascension with delight, as if part of himself were attached to them and were now swinging in space.

Now it seemed to Michael that this divorce which happened every day would stretch intolerably during the rest of their time together, and he was wishing for the night, for darkness.

A blind couple passed them, leaning on each other. Michael envied them. (How I envy the blind who can love in the dark. Never to see the eye of the lover without reflection or remembrance. Black moment of desire knowing nothing of the being one is holding but the fiery point in darkness at which they could touch and spark. Blind lovers throwing themselves in the void of desire lying together for a night without dawn. Never to see the day upon the body that was taken. Could love go further in the darkness? Further and deeper without awakening to the sorrows of lucidity? Touch only warm flesh and listen only to the warmth of a voice!)

There was no darkness dark enough to prevent Michael from seeing the eyes of the lover turning away, empty of remembrance, never dark enough not to see the death of a love, the defect of a love, the end of the night of desire.

No love blind enough for him to escape the sorrows of lucidity.

"And now," said Donald, his arms full of presents, "let's go to the café."

Elbows touching, toes overlapping, breaths mingling, they sat in circles in the café while the passers-by flowed down the boulevard, the flower vendors plied their bouquets, the newsboys sang their street songs, and the evening achieved the marriage of day and night called twilight.

An organ grinder was playing at the corner like a fountain of mechanical birds singing wildly Carmen's provocations in this artificial paradise of etiolated trees, while the monkey rattled his chains and the pennies fell in the tin cup.

They sat rotating around each other like nearsighted planets, they sat mutating, exchanging personalities.

Jay seemed the one nearest to the earth, for there was the dew of pleasure upon his lips, there was this roseate bloom of content on his cheeks because he was nearest to the earth. He could possess the world physically whenever he wished, he could bite into it, eat it, digest it without difficulty. He had an ample appetite, he was not discriminating, he had a good digestion. So his face shone with the solid colors of Dutch paintings, with the blood tones of a well-nourished man, in a world never far from his teeth, never made invisible or unsubstantial, for he carried no inner chamber in which the present scene must repeat itself for the commentator.

He carried no inner chamber in which this scene must

be stored in order to be possessed. He carried no echo and no retentions. No snail roof around his body, no veils, no insulators.

His entrances and exists were as fluid, mobile, facile, as his drinking and its consequences. For him there was no sense of space between human beings, no distance to traverse, no obstacles to overcome to reach one another, no effort to make.

Because of his confidence in the natural movements of the planets, a pattern all arranged beforehand by some humorous astrologer, he always showed a smiling face in this lantern slide of life in Paris, and felt no strings of bondage, of restraint, and no tightrope walking as the others did.

From the first moment when he had cut utterly the umbilical cord between himself and his mother by running away from home at the age of fourteen and never once returning, he had known this absence of spools, lassos, webs, safety nets. He had eluded them all.

Thus in the sky of the café tables rotating, the others circled around him to drink of his gaiety, hoping to catch his secret formula.

Was it because he had accepted that such an indifference to effort led men to the edge of the river, to sleep under bridges, was it because he had decided that he did not mind sleeping under bridges, drinking from the fountain, smoking cigarette butts, eating soup from the soup line of the Hospital de la Sante?

Was this his secret? To relinquish, to dispossess one's self of all wishes, to renounce, to be attached to no one, to hold no dream, to live in a state of anarchy?

Actually he never reached the last stage. He always met someone who assumed the responsibility of his existence.

But he could sense whoever unwound from the center of a spool and rewound himself back into it again at night, or the one who sought to lasso the loved one into an indissoluble spiral, or the one who flung himself from heights intent on catching the swing midway and fearful of a fatal slip into abysms.

This always incited him to grasp giant scissors and cut through all the patterns.

He began to open people before the café table as he opened bottles, not delicately, not gradually, but un-corking them, hurling direct questions at them like javelins, assaulting them with naked curiosity.

A secret, an evasion, a shrinking, drove him to repeat his thrusts like one hard of hearing: what did you say?

No secrets! No mystifications allowed! Spill open! Give yourself publicly like those fanatics who confess to the community.

He hated withdrawals, shells, veils. They aroused the barbarian in him, the violator of cities, the sacker and invader.

Dive from any place whatever!

But dive!

With large savage scissors he cut off all the moorings. Cut off responsibilities, families, shelters. He sent every one of them towards the open sea, into chaos, into poverty, into solitude, into storms.

At first they bounced safely on the buoyant mattress of his enthusiams. Jay became gayer and gayer as his timid passengers embarked on unfamiliar and tumultous seas.

Some felt relieved to have been violated. There was no other way to open their beings. They were glad to have been done violence to as secrets have a way of corroding their containers. Others felt ravaged like invaded countries, felt hopelessly exhibited and ashamed of this lesser aspect of themselves.

As soon as Jay had emptied the person, and the bottle, of all it contained, down to the sediments, he was satiated.

Come, said Jay, display the worst in yourself. To laugh

it is necessary to present a charade of our diminished states. To face the natural man, and the charm of his defects. Come, said Jay, let us share our flaws together. I do not believe in heroes. I believe in the natural man.

(I now know the secret of Jay's well-being, thought Lillian. *He does not care.* That is his secret. He does not care! And I shall never learn this from him. I will never be able to feel as he does. I must run away from him. I will return to New York.)

And at this thought, the cord she had imagined tying her and Jay together for eternity, the cord of marriage, taut with incertitude, worn with anxiety, snapped, and she felt unmoored.

While he unmoored others, by cutting through the knots of responsibilities, he had inadvertently cut the binding, choking cord between them. From the moment she decided to sail away from him she felt elated.

All these tangled cords, from the first to the last, from the mother to the husband, to the children, and to Jay, all dissolved at once, and Jay was surprised to hear Lillian laugh in a different tone, for most times her laughter had a rusty quality which brought it closer to a sob, as if she had never determined which she intended to do.

At the same hour at the tip of the Observatory astronomers were tabulating mileage between planets, and just as Djuna had learned to measure such mileage by the oscillations of her heart (he is warm and near, he is remote and cool) from her first experience with Michael, past master in the art of creating distance between human beings, Michael himself arrived with Donald and she could see instantly that he was suffering from his full awareness of the impenetrable distance between himself and Donald, between himself and the world of adolescence he wanted to remain in forever and from which his lack of playfulness and recklessness barred him.

As soon as Michael saw Djuna's eyes he had the feeling of being restored to visibility, as if by gazing into the clear mirrors of her compassion he were reincarnated, for the relentless work accomplished by Donald's exclusion of him from his boyish world deprived him of his very existence.

Djuna needed only to say: Hello, Michael! for him to feel he was no longer a kindly protective ghost necessary to Donald's existence. For Djuna saw him handsome, gifted in astronomy and mathematics, rich with many knowledges, eloquent when properly warmed.

Hello, Michael! Djuna said, and the 100000000000 000000000 miles between himself and human beings

170

became like a small pencil addition on a note paper and not a state of being. They were laid aside like a student's abstractions, and now he was sitting in a café and Donald at his right was merely a very beautiful boy of which there were so many, cut out like a clay pigeon at the fair, with only a façade, and that is what Djuna had called him from the very beginning (the first time she had said it he had been angry and brooded on the insufferable jealousy of woman). Hello, Michael! How is your clay pigeon today?

Such fine threads passed between Michael and Djuna. He could always seize the intermediary color of her mood. That was his charm, his quality, this fine incision from his knowledge of woman, this capacity for dealing in essences.

This love without possibility of incarnation which took place between Djuna and all the descendants of Michael, the lineage of these carriers of subtleties known only to men of his race.

They had found a territory which existed beyond sensual countries, and by a communion of swift words could charm each other actively in spite of the knowledge that this enchantment would have no ordinary culmination.

"Djuna," said Michael, "I see all your thoughts running in all directions, like minnows."

Then immediately he knew this in her was a symptom of anxiety, and he avoided the question which would have wounded her: "Has Paul's father sent him to India?"

For in the way she sat there he knew she was awaiting a mortal blow.

At this moment there appeared on the marble-topped tables the stains of drink, the sediments and dregs of false beatitudes.

At this moment the organ grinder changed his tune, and ceased to shower the profligacies of Carmen.

The laughter of Pagliacci bleached by city fumes, wailed like a loon out of the organ, so that the monkey cornered by a joviality which had neither a sound of man or monkey rattled his chains in greater desperation and saluted with his red Turkish hat every stranger who might deliver him from this loud-speaker tree to which he had been tied.

He danced a pleading dance to be delivered from this tree from which the twisting of a handle brought forth black birds of corrugated melodies.

But as the pennies fell he remembered his responsibilities, his prayer for silent trees vanished from his eyes as he attempted a gesture of gratitude with his red Turkish hat.

Djuna walked back again into her labyrinthian cities of the interior.

Where music bears no titles flowing like a subterranean river carrying all the moods, sensations and impressions into dissolutions forming and reforming a world in terms of flow . . .

where houses wear but façades exposed to easy entrances and exits

where streets do not bear a name because they are the streets of secret sorrows

where the birds who sing are the birds of peace, the birds of paradise, the colored birds of desire which appear in our dreams

there are those who feared to be lost in this voyage without compass, barometers, steering wheel or encyclopedias

but Djuna knew that at this surrender of the self began a sinking into deeper layers of awareness deeper and deeper starting at the topsoil of gaiety and descending through the geological stairways carrying only the delicate weighing machine of the heart to weigh the imponderable through these streets of secret sorrows in which the music was anonymous and people lost their identities to better be carried and swept back and forth through the years to find only the points of ecstasy . . .

registering only the dates and titles of emotion which alone enters the flesh and lodges itself against the flux and loss of memory

that only the important dates of deep feeling may recur again and again each time anew through the wells, fountains and rivers of music. . . .